DEVYN'S DREAM

BOOK 3 - HEARTSGATE HEALING

KAY P. DAWSON

CHAPTER 1

"Is there anything else missing that you need me to add into my report?"

Devyn's eyes held those of the kind policeman who was holding a notepad in front of his chest, waiting for her answer.

"No, officer. I think I've given you everything I can think of."

He looked down at his notes and read it over to himself. "And do you know where we could find your brother, to question him about his involvement? I'll do my best to find everything for you, but unless we can find any of the stolen property on him, it'll be hard to prove it was him."

Devyn nodded, swallowing the lump in her

throat that threatened her ability to speak. "I understand."

He lifted his head and gave her a warm smile. She wished he wasn't being so nice to her because it was making it even harder to hold herself together. She could see the pity in his eyes and right now, she was feeling angry enough at herself, without having everyone else in the world know how gullible she'd been.

"Don't you worry, miss. I'm going to do everything I can to find your things and get them back to you. You've given me enough information to go on to question him and hopefully get some answers. You didn't do anything wrong by trusting him."

Her chin shook as she fought back the tears. "Thank you."

She watched as the older man and his partner walked out the door, closing it behind them, leaving her standing in the middle of her living room alone. She hugged her arms around herself tight as she let the tears finally fall. Her orange tomcat, Jasper, came over and rubbed against her leg, sensing she needed his attention.

How could she have been so naive? She'd been so desperate to have a "real" family and finding her brother had been a dream come true for her. But the past few weeks had quickly shattered that dream.

She had tried hard to make it work, and to get him the help he needed for his addictions, but she quickly learned he wasn't ready for anything she could give him.

Well, except of course, the money and property he'd stolen from her today to pay his drug debts off.

Lowering herself to the couch, she leaned back into the soft cushions and rested her head, looking up at the ceiling. Jasper jumped up and came over to lie beside her, resting his head on her leg as he looked up, waiting for her to acknowledge him. Her life hadn't been an easy one, but she'd never felt so betrayed or used before. And the worst part was, she had no one to blame but herself.

She had overlooked the problems, not wanting to admit things weren't going to turn out perfectly like she'd always hoped they would if she found her family.

A knock on the door startled her, setting her pulse racing. Was it her brother coming back? Or, one of his "friends" looking for more?

"Devyn, dear, it's Doctor Lachele. You weren't at Book Club this evening, so I just wanted to stop by and check that everything is all right. You know I get a sense about things."

Devyn smiled to herself, despite the turmoil in her heart. Dr. Lachele had become a light in her life, not just with her "magic" but with her ability to just know when someone needed a shoulder.

Going over to the door, she opened it wide, and at the sight of the kind, purple-haired woman smiling at her, she completely broke down in tears.

"Oh, my dear. Let's get inside and figure this out. You come with me and tell me what's troubling you." Dr. Lachele put an arm around her shoulders and led her back to the couch, sitting down beside her and wrapping her arms around her. "I just knew something wasn't right, so I'm glad I came over."

Devyn let herself cry for the loss she'd suffered today. It wasn't the material things she was upset about. It was the chance to have the family she'd dreamed about.

"Why do I get the feeling this has something to do with the brother you let into your life?"

Dr. Lachele had warned her a few weeks ago about a bad feeling she had about Darryl. But Devyn hadn't wanted to listen. She'd been too sure that now they'd found each other, he would turn his life around and get on the straight and narrow.

Even as she'd tried to convince Dr. Lachele about it, Devyn could admit to herself now, that even she'd had her doubts. She just hadn't wanted to face them at the time.

"He stole the money I had saved up in the little box in my closet. I know I should have put it into the bank, but this was the money for a trip to see all the sights along the Oregon Trail. And now, knowing my friends would have seen those sights in real time had made it all the more exciting for me." She pulled back and wiped at her eyes, unable to meet Dr. Lachele's gaze. "He'd been begging me for money for days because he said he owed his old drug dealer. I gave him some yesterday to pay it off, and he walked into my room when I was putting the box back in my closet."

She swallowed hard and sighed. "I guess he decided he needed more."

Shaking her head angrily, she stood up and turned to face Dr. Lachele. "He told me he was getting clean and wanted a new start. Once he had this last debt paid off, he'd be able to start over and we could be a family." She snorted loudly and turned, walking over to the window. "Once again, Devyn Carr makes stupid decisions because she's naive and gullible."

"Now, Devyn. Don't be saying things like that. There's nothing wrong with being the sort of person who has a kind heart and wants to believe the best in people. The world would be a lot better place if everyone was like that. You believed your brother was able to change, and maybe someday he will see the mistakes he made. But, it's not your place to make him see that. You did what you could. Now, you need to worry about yourself. You deserve better than sitting around waiting for something that may never happen."

Devyn turned around at the sound of her phone buzzing. Looking down at the screen, a number she didn't recognize was texting her. Her heart sank as she read the words.

Where's your brother? He was s'posed to pay me back today, but didn't show. I need my money. I'll get it from you one way or another.

The blood drained from her face as she read it aloud to Dr. Lachele.

"What am I going to do?"

Her voice was barely above a whisper. Fear wrapped around her chest as she tried to keep her hands from trembling. She didn't know who it was texting her, but it didn't matter. They were all the same. All the people her brother associated with were the kind who didn't care who they hurt, as long as they got paid.

And now, she was about to become collateral damage to her brother's lifestyle.

Dr. Lachele walked over and reached out to take her hands in hers, holding them steady. "You don't need to stay here and deal with problems that aren't yours anymore, Devyn. What is the one thing you've always dreamed of?"

Devyn held her gaze. "Having family."

"And, you thought you'd found that with your brother. But maybe you were so busy hoping for something to be true, you didn't see what you already had."

"Jenna and Carly."

Her two best friends. The ones who had always been with her, ever since they were young girls in the foster system in New York. They'd always been there for each other.

But, when the purple-haired Dr. Lachele, with strange, magical powers had shown up at book club a few months ago, things had changed. She had the ability to send people to whatever time they wanted to go to, and both her friends had gone off to find true love.

And Dr. Lachele had assured her that both were happy and content in their choices.

Devyn hadn't ever thought about going herself, not really giving much thought to finding love for herself. At the time, she'd just found her brother and was excited for the chance to have a real family.

"I don't really know if I'm looking for someone to fall in love with. But I do miss my friends." She looked at Dr. Lachele with a spark of hope she was starting to feel ignite inside her.

"My dear, sometimes what you're looking for is right under your nose. And sometimes, the things you don't think you're even dreaming about will fall into your lap without you even expecting it."

Devyn smiled at the woman in front of her. She always had a lot of wisdom to impart, even if most of the time Devyn didn't really understand it.

"Can I go to where they are? Even if I'm not going for a love match?"

Dr. Lachele tilted her head back and laughed. "Oh, Devyn. There aren't any rules to my 'magic,' as you girls always call it. I'm Doctor Lachele. I make my own rules."

And with that, Devyn knew exactly what she was going to do. She wasn't going to spend the rest of her life looking over her shoulder because of choices her brother had made. He didn't care about having a real relationship with her.

So, she was going to be with the only people who ever had truly been a family to her. And if she happened to find someone to fall in love with, she wouldn't be upset about that either.

CHAPTER 2

Luke leaned back against the large rock he'd placed his bed next to and stared up at the dark sky. No matter how many nights he sat and did the same thing, he never got over the amazement he felt when seeing the stars going for miles and miles beyond the horizon. He wondered, like he did every time, at the vastness of the sky beyond their own world.

He stretched his legs, and arched his back until it cracked, loosening some of the knots he'd accumulated over the day in the saddle. Even after all these weeks on the trail, he still felt the effects by the time the wagon train stopped every night.

This was the third time he'd signed on to captain an outfit heading west, so he was confident in his ability to get them to Oregon safely. So far, they'd lost a few travelers to disease and illness, as well as some accidents along the way. But he knew it was part of the job, even if it did still bother him every time they lost another life. He had learned to bottle it up and hold his feelings in when it came to death.

As he stared up at the sky, the feelings that came every night when he was alone with his thoughts started to come through. He'd given up trying to fight them long ago, knowing it was his punishment that he would live with for the rest of his life.

Guilt over the death of his wife and child would consume him until the day he was called home too.

The smiling face of Josephine creeped into his thoughts, bringing a smile to his face even as the pain took over his heart. As he held her image in his mind, he tried to see the face of the baby he'd held for such a short time. It had faded with time, but he could still feel the small weight in his arms as he'd said goodbye to the tiny body that hadn't survived the birth.

And within the hour, his child's mother had joined him, leaving Luke alone to live with the guilt of surviving.

For months after, he drifted through his days not caring if he lived or died. He'd known Josephine was delicate. She'd never been strong, and he'd been sure over the months they were married to always take care of her the best he could. He let the ache in his heart consume him as he remembered the times he'd become frustrated with her when she couldn't do so many of the things he knew other women could do.

But Josephine had been pampered her whole life, so he'd had to remind himself often that it wasn't her fault. The fact she had even agreed to marry him, someone who was "beneath" her station in life, had always amazed him. And he'd done his best to continue pampering her the way she deserved.

He should have never made her leave the city where there were more amenities and better doctors to take care of a pregnant woman. She'd ended up paying the price with her life because by the time the old country doctor had finally arrived at their house, it was too late to do much. The baby had been coming out the wrong way, and there wasn't anything he could do.

Luke lowered his head into his hands. The coolness of the night air whispered around him, trying to bring him back to now. But he wasn't going to let it. The least he could do for Josephine and his baby was spend the rest of his days feeling the pain of their death.

Looking up, he found his eyes moving toward the camp where Adam and Jenna were set up. Hunter and Carly were beside them with their daughter Mary, and he found himself smiling as he watched Hunter lift the sleeping child and carry her over to the wagon.

He rolled his eyes as he spotted Gordon, the large dog that was always underfoot, sit up straight and look directly at him. He hadn't thought he'd made a noise but obviously it had been enough for Gordon to think he must have been calling him over. He laughed softly as the dog plodded over and then sat right next to him, leaning in to make sure Luke gave him some attention.

"Gordon, you're supposed to be keeping an eye on Mary when she goes to bed. I don't need you over here." But he still affectionately scratched the dog behind his ears as he let himself enjoy the company.

He was grateful for Adam and Hunter, and their families, for allowing him to be included in meals with them and so much more over the past few weeks on the trail. They'd entrusted him with secrets he wasn't sure he was really convinced about the truth of, but he was glad they felt he was trustworthy enough to share.

Everything about the day Carly and Hunter were

married still had him a bit confused, and while Adam had tried explaining things to him on the ride back from the fort, Luke still couldn't believe the truth of it.

Adam had told him that both Jenna and Carly were from the future, and somehow, they'd been able to come back to this time to find the men they were meant to be with.

Luke had outright laughed at the story, even while he tried to make sense out of the strange purple-haired woman who'd shown up in the middle of nowhere, then quickly vanished just as easily. They'd tried to explain how she was the "matchmaker."

Whenever he tried to come up with some other explanation, though, for how both Jenna and Carly had somehow ended up on a wagon train bound for Oregon, in the ways they had, he just couldn't find any other reasonable explanation.

So, he'd gone along with their story, even if it was a bit ridiculous to believe.

"Am I supposed to believe you're from the future too, Gordon? You don't look like a future-dog to me." He smiled down at the upturned face that looked up at him, enjoying the attention.

Suddenly, the hair on Gordon's neck stood up as

his eyes moved past Luke into the darkness behind them. A low growl started in his throat, making Luke sit up straight and turn to see what had caught the dog's attention.

The men who'd been assigned the night watch would be keeping an eye on the livestock for any wild animals or threats, but Luke also knew sometimes it was hard to see everything happening around them in the dark.

He leaned forward as Gordon slowly walked into the darkness beyond where Luke had laid out his bedding, trying to get his eyes to focus on whatever had drawn the dog's attention.

"Jasper! Get back here!"

Luke leaped to his feet, his heart pounding as a woman's voice shouted from the darkness. Before he had a chance to react, something small and orange tore past him, with Gordon taking off after it.

"What the—?"

The rest of his words were cut off as a woman raced into his line of vision, almost knocking him over as she desperately tried to catch up to whatever had already run past him.

He reached out to steady himself before giving his head a shake, trying to comprehend what was happening.

"Jasper, please! Gordon, stop chasing him." The woman was trying to grab hold of the dog but Gordon was determined to catch whatever the ball of fur was that had dared to intrude in his territory.

A few of the travelers were starting to wake up, rousing themselves to see what the commotion was about. But Gordon wasn't paying them any attention, having chased his prey into the back of Hunter's wagon, where he was now standing with his front legs resting on the frame while he barked loudly into the void beyond the canvas.

Carly ran over and pulled Gordon back from the wagon, scolding him for the noise he was making. "Shush, Gordon. You're going to wake the whole camp up. What is wrong with you?"

"Carly?"

Luke had made his way over to the wagons and watched in confusion as Carly turned with her mouth wide open, then reached out and grabbed the strange woman in an embrace.

"Devyn! Is it really you?" She pulled back and stared at the woman as tears started flowing down her cheeks. "I can't believe you're here! What are you doing? I thought you were staying with your brother."

By now, Gordon had gone back to the opening in

the wagon where Mary was peeking out, rubbing at her eyes from being woken so suddenly.

"Carly? There's a cute little kitty that jumped in here, and he's scared of Gordon's barking."

Carly was still holding onto the arms of the other woman, and she laughed quickly. "Of course, you brought Jasper with you."

The rest of the family had come over now, and when Jenna saw the new woman, she started crying too. The three women stood hugging each other and laughing while the men were left standing and watching in shock.

Luke looked to Hunter, who was standing closest to him. "Do you have any idea what is going on?"

Hunter laughed and shrugged as he crossed his arms in front of his chest. "Well, Luke, I'd say you've just met another friend of Carly and Jenna's. And, whether you choose to believe it or not, I think it's quite possible she's come here from the future too."

CHAPTER 3

"Oh, you poor thing. You must be terrified." Devyn took Jasper from Carly's outstretched hands, pulling him in close to her chest, while Gordon continued to sniff at him. He'd finally stopped barking while Carly had crawled up into the wagon to retrieve the scared cat from among the belongings being carried inside.

A handsome man reached up and lifted Carly easily out of the back of the wagon, setting her onto the ground beside him. Devyn smiled, realizing this had to be the man Carly had been matched with.

"Your kitty is so cute. He can stay here in the wagon with me if you want until he gets used to being around Gordon."

Devyn looked down at the orange cat who was

now hissing at the dog. Poor Jasper. Being dragged across decades just because she couldn't imagine living without him. What was she thinking bringing a pampered cat out here in the wilderness? How was she possibly going to look after him and keep him safe?

"Devyn, this is Mary." Carly motioned toward the little girl who was peeking out of the back of the wagon. "And, this is her uncle, Hunter." The way Carly reached over and held onto Hunter's arm, smiling up into his face warmly, left no doubt who he was to her.

"It's very nice to meet you, Mary. If you don't mind looking after Jasper, I would very much appreciate it. He's pretty scared out here. So, I'm sure he would love to snuggle up with you inside the wagon." She set the terrified cat back into the wagon, where he scrambled to the front to hide behind a crate. "You might just need to give him some time to get used to you and not be so scared."

The little girl giggled as she tucked her head back inside the canvas. "Don't worry. I'll look after him and keep him from being scared."

Jenna reached out and took her hand, leading her toward the man beside her. "And, Devyn, this is my husband, Adam."

Devyn nodded in greeting at the other hand-some man smiling at her. "Jenna has told me a lot about you, Devyn. But she hadn't mentioned anything about the possibility of you joining us here."

Devyn laughed sharply, hoping it didn't sound as bitter to everyone else's ears as it did to hers. "Well, I hadn't really planned on it, but life had other ideas."

Her gaze fell on the lone man standing off to the side watching everything intently. She had seen him when she first "woke up" from being sent here. Everything had been a bit fuzzy in her mind, and it was so dark she could barely see beyond her own face. Before she had much of a chance to compre-hend where she was exactly, Jasper had jumped from her arms and run away, with Carly's dog hot on his heels.

His eyes were on hers now, while he patiently waited for everyone to go through their reunion. But she had a feeling he was watching everything closely, trying to take it all in.

"Oh, Devyn! You have to meet the captain of this wagon train." Jenna tugged on her arm again, and before she'd been moved closer to the man, she caught Carly smirking at her out of the corner of her eye.

"Luke, this is our friend, Devyn Carr. Devyn, this is *Luke Bryan*."

Devyn's mouth dropped open, and she choked on her words. Her head slowly turned toward her friends who both looked back at her with wide grins.

Everyone who knew Devyn, knew about her unhealthy crush on country singer Luke Bryan. It wasn't a secret how she'd been adamant her entire life the only man she would ever marry was Luke Bryan.

But it had been a joke. Not just the fact that the real Luke Bryan was already married, but there was also the whole him being a famous country music star who would never notice someone like her.

"Somehow, I'm not surprised in the least by your reaction. It's about the same as both of your friend's when they heard my name."

The man put his hand out to hers, and she took it, nodding as she tried to think of something to say. The worst part of it all was, she realized this man in front of her not only shared a name with Luke Bryan, but he had a lot of his features too.

If she didn't know better, she would have sworn the star had been brought back in time with her.

Except she had to admit to herself that this Luke Bryan had an even more rugged look that could only come from living life on the frontier. His blue eyes held hers, forcing her to swallow hard as she tried to get words to come from her mouth.

"I'm sorry. It's just that your name is the same as someone else..." How would she say it? She didn't know the real Luke Bryan. And she was sure he wouldn't understand anything about what a famous country music singer was in this time period.

Not only that...but exactly how much did Luke know about where Carly and Jenna had come from?

"Yes, I've heard that." His eyes moved around the group gathered by the wagon. "And I assume you've come here from the same place as Jenna and Carly?" He looked directly back at her and waited for her answer.

Thankfully, Carly replied for her. "I know it's hard for you to believe it all, Luke. But you saw what happened that day by the fort. When Doctor Lachele showed up. And you really can't explain any other way how Hunter and Adam found me and Gordon lying in the middle of the prairies."

Carly came over and took hold of Devyn's arm, smiling warmly at her. "I've known Devyn my whole life. She comes from the same time as Jenna and me. Saying goodbye to her was the hardest thing I had to do when I came here, so you have no idea how happy I am to see her here too."

He clenched his jaw, and in the low light from the campfire, she watched as he closed his eyes and pressed his hands to his head.

"You realize just how hard this is to believe? I know a lot has happened during this trip I have trouble explaining, but to hear that you ladies have come here from a time in the future is difficult to comprehend. How will we explain her sudden appearance to the others?"

Devyn met his gaze, and she found herself holding her breath. For some reason, even though she felt guilty for putting him in the position of having to explain her arrival here in the middle of nowhere, she also knew he'd find a way.

In all her life, she'd never really met a man who made her feel like he would take care of things and she could trust him, so it was an unfamiliar feeling.

"I guess we can say she came on at Fort Boise when we stopped. We will say she was suffering from an illness that kept her in the wagon for the past couple of days." He looked around as he worked out the plan in his mind.

"I'm sorry for making things a bit difficult. I promise I won't get in anyone's way. I made sure

Doctor Lachele sent me with my own warm blankets and some food, so I won't take away from anyone else. It's all still over by where I woke up."

"Oh, Devyn. You're not going to be any trouble at all! You can travel with us and sleep over by our wagons at night. I'm just so happy we're all here, together again!" Jenna threw her arms around Devyn, and Carly joined in.

She squeezed her eyes tight, and held her friends close, so happy to be with them again. She didn't care if she never found the true love they had found by making this journey. As long as she had them, she was content.

But, when she opened her eyes and met the blue stare of the man by the wagon watching her so closely, she had to admit to a slight tingle that made her wonder if just maybe, there might be a chance for her too.

Surely, Dr. Lachele wouldn't have made it this easy, would she?

CHAPTER 4

"Well, I have to give you credit for guiding us all this way in such good time. It's been a challenge, and many situations most wagon train captains wouldn't have had to deal with, so we owe you a great deal of gratitude."

Luke took a sip of his coffee and shrugged. "Nothing more than what I was paid to do. Besides, we still have a ways to go before we reach Oregon City. In a few days, we're going to have to cross back over the Snake River, and I'm sure you know by now how tense these river crossings can be. I just want to get everyone to their destination without too many incidents."

"I've read about these river crossings. Will this one be dangerous?"

Luke glanced over at the black-haired woman who sat on a crate across the fire from him. Devyn's eyes were wide as they discussed the upcoming river crossing. She'd only been with them for a few days now, and he had to admit a certain curiosity toward her. He told himself it was simply because she was still trying to settle in, and he knew she was struggling with a few of the challenges that came with life on a wagon train.

He wasn't prepared to let himself admit how beautiful she was. Or the fact, that despite the challenges she was facing, she was meeting each of them head-on without any complaints. She wasn't like many of the women he'd known in his life.

"River crossings always have risk, but we've done a few now, so I hope most of the travelers will be prepared." He wasn't going to tell her there had been a few casualties during the past crossings because he didn't need her worrying about it. It was a fact of life out here, and everyone knew the risks.

Devyn looked down at the cat sleeping peacefully in her lap as she stroked behind his ears. Luke still couldn't believe the cat hadn't run off at the first chance it had. He'd never seen any animal so docile in his entire life. It had even seemed to form some kind of strange bond with Gordon, and he'd found himself laughing to himself many times as he came across the two animals walking alongside the wagons throughout the day.

"Well, I for one can't wait to get to Oregon and finally see my sister-in-law after all these years. It's been too long on this dirty, hot trail and I'm ready to have an actual roof over my head again." Adam's mother, Minnie, sat with her knitting as she often did after the evening meal. She was a strong woman and had made every day on the trail a little easier for everyone. "In Anna's last letter, she couldn't say enough about the little community where they've settled and put down roots. And there are still plenty of opportunities all around the area for anyone else willing to put in a bit of work."

Adam was sitting on the ground next to Jenna, and he leaned back and rested on his elbows as he looked up at the darkening sky above them. "First thing I'll be doing is building a nice little house for us. My cousin Connor has a blacksmith's shop there, and has said he'll welcome the help, so I'll be glad to be back working at what I'm meant to be doing."

"Me too. I'm going to find some land and get a crop in the ground next spring. It'll be tough going, especially since it will be almost winter by the time we arrive, but just the thought of getting back out on the land is enough to get me excited again." Hunter put his arm around Carly and smiled down at her.

Mary had already been put to sleep for the night in the wagon, but Luke felt a familiar tug of jealousy in his chest as he watched the little family in front of him. They would all be making a new home and life together in Oregon, something Luke had thought he had for himself back in Kansas, all those years ago.

"What about you, Luke? What are your plans after this trip?"

Minnie was smiling warmly at him, making him wish he knew the answer to give her. For some reason, his eyes moved toward Devyn who was watching him closely.

"Haven't given it much thought. Likely spend some time in Oregon before making my way back east again to lead more travelers next year."

"Surely you must have some family around to visit and let them know how you're doing. Don't you get tired of always traveling without settling down?"

"Ma, what Luke chooses to do with his life is no concern of ours."

Adam gently scolded his mother as he rolled his eyes in Luke's direction. "I apologize for my mother who tends to have her nose in places where it doesn't belong."

Luke chuckled at the stern look Minnie sent her son. "I do not put my nose anywhere. I'm just curious and since Luke has taken such good care of us, I want to make sure he's just as happy when we reach the end of the trail as we are." She looked over at Luke with a serious look. "I just hate to think of you being alone so much. A man your age should be starting a family and settling down."

"Ma…" Adam sent a warning glance in her direction, and Luke almost laughed out loud at the stare down the two of them were now having.

He put his hand up in Adam's direction. "It's all right, Adam. You're lucky to have a ma who cares so much about everyone. I lost my own ma when I was young and was raised by my father. He passed some time ago, so there's just me left." He shrugged, hoping no one could see the loneliness he felt deep in his soul. "I was married briefly, but unfortunately my wife died, so now it's just easier for me to travel around the country and not have anyone to look after but myself."

He sensed the sadness that had fallen over the group as they listened to him, and he cringed inwardly, wondering why he'd even brought any of that up. He hadn't really opened up to anyone for a long time, but this group of people had become the closest thing he'd felt to a family in years.

Before anyone could reply, Mary's head peered out from the canvas on the wagon. "My brain is too busy to sleep. Can't I stay up and visit with everyone? It's too lonely in here by myself. When will Jasper get to come to bed?"

Hunter laughed and walked over to the back of the wagon. "Mary, you've had a long day and another long one tomorrow, so you need your sleep. We're all going to bed soon too."

Her bottom lip stuck out, and she sighed loudly to make sure everyone knew how unhappy she was about it. Devyn stood up and carried Jasper over to her, holding the cat up to the little girl. "Here you go, Mary. Jasper is tired now too, so he's ready to snuggle in with you. Make sure you take good care of him for me."

The cat had been sleeping in the wagon at night with Mary since they got here, in order to keep it from becoming prey to any wild animals around them. Luke shook his head as he once again wondered what Devyn was thinking bringing a cat along on a journey like this.

He knew if she'd arrived here in the beginning with it, there's no way the animal would have made it to Oregon. But he hoped he could keep it safe for the remaining few weeks they had on the trail.

Although the more he got to see of Devyn, the more he realized she likely wouldn't need his help with much of anything. And it was a feeling he wasn't used to.

But he also knew the safest option was to keep his distance from her anyway. Because she had somehow drawn his attention in a way he hadn't had with a woman in a very long time.

And that wasn't something he was ready to even try to understand.

CHAPTER 5

"Oh, you guys. I don't know how you've managed to walk all this way. I've only been doing this a few days now and I'm ready to throw in the towel. And I don't care how much you tell me I will get used to it. I will never, *ever* feel comfortable without the convenience of a flush toilet out here. Not to mention a nice shower every day."

Devyn reached up and wiped at the dust around her eyes, turning her head slightly to make sure Jasper was keeping up with them. Although she wasn't sure why she worried. He'd settled into a nice routine of running back and forth, playing with Gordon and Mary, or chasing critters he found along the way. And, when he got tired, he would simply jump up into the back of the closest wagon and sleep the afternoon away.

Carly laughed before reaching down and picking up a buffalo "chip." "Trust me, it's still really hard to live with. But at least the days are cooling down a bit now, so it's not as bad. And I've learned to enjoy the quick rinses I get in the creeks or rivers along the way."

Jenna nodded in agreement. "I've gone through almost all the scented bodywash I brought with me, so I'm going to soon need Doctor Lachele to bring me some more. If I'd known you were coming…"

"Well, it's not like I could send you all a letter announcing my intentions. Besides, I really didn't decide until just before I showed up here. I thought it was best not to let myself have too much time to think about it."

She scratched the top of her head, wishing she could rip the bonnet off and let her hair "breathe." But she knew this was likely the better option to avoid being sunburned, even with the sunscreen Jenna had.

"Remind me again why you guys decided to come to a time on the Oregon Trail? Surely you could have just gone to a place already settled where at least an outhouse was available, and a tub to bring some warm water in to wash with. Not to mention being in a house at night, and walking hundreds of miles wearing more clothes at once than we normally would have worn in a week." Devyn loosened the top button on the sturdy dress she'd worn, making a mental note to be sure it was done back up if a man came along. Out here, the poor thing would likely think she was a trollop if she dared show any amount of skin.

Her eyes moved to Luke who rode ahead of the wagons. He was far away, but she could see the broad shoulders moving as he gently guided his horse along the trail.

She wondered what he'd do if he saw her showing a little extra skin?

"So, do you think Luke is the one you've been sent here for?"

Devyn choked as she swallowed a mouthful of dust, not prepared for the question from Jenna. Both of her friends grinned in her direction, waiting for her reply.

"That seems a bit too obvious, don't you think? I don't believe Doctor Lachele works that way. Besides, I told her I didn't even care if I was being sent to find my perfect match. I just wanted to be back together with my friends, even if I end up living alone and becoming a crazy, old spinster."

But she found her gaze moving back to the man on the horse, and her cheeks burned as she realized he was staring at her too. She wouldn't be sad if Luke was the reason she was here, but she wasn't going to let it consume her thoughts. Maybe Dr. Lachele had someone better in mind for her, if she had truly sent her here for a love match. Luke was nice to look at, and he did share the name with someone she'd already loved for a long time. And he obviously was a considerate man who took his job seriously.

If he'd shown any kind of interest in her as a woman, she might think he was the one. But when she'd heard the pain in his voice as he'd spoken about his deceased wife, she knew it wasn't something he would likely be completely over. And the last thing she wanted was to be some kind of second choice or rebound relationship. He might just have too much baggage coming with him.

And Lord knows, she was bringing enough of her own. Which was why she really didn't care too much if she wasn't here for a love match. She was used to being on her own, so it wasn't like she'd have to learn how to do that.

"I'm glad you came here to be with us, Devyn, but I'm sure Doctor Lachele wouldn't have agreed to just send you somewhere to be with your friends. We all know how that crazy, purple-haired lady works. She's always got something up her sleeve."

Devyn sidestepped a piece of buffalo dung, and grimaced when Jenna reached down to pick it up and put it in her outstretched apron in front of her. When she caught her friend's eye, they both started to laugh.

"Don't you dare say a word! I know what you're thinking…"

Carly joined in the laughter as she reached down to pick up another piece. "Trust me, Devyn, you'll to be doing the same things as we are soon. I know there was a time none of us would have ever been caught doing something like this, but obviously we've had to learn to adapt. You should ask Jenna about her first time milking Annie."

The women shared in the laughter as Jenna recounted the story of almost being trampled to death by a cow. And now had become friends with that same cow. Something none of them ever could have imagined would be a real thing happening in any of their lives.

"It does a heart good to hear the laughter of

women, especially during these difficult days on the trail."

Devyn turned to face the man who had walked over to join them from a few wagons back. She'd noticed him a few times because he was extremely tall, and always wore a suit which seemed out of place on the trail. He tipped his hat in her direction. She quickly brought her hands to her chest to redo the button up.

"I haven't had the fortune of meeting you since you joined the wagon train back at the fort. I hope you're feeling much better. I am Mr. Andrews, Esquire."

They had all stopped walking now, while introductions could be made. "Mr. Andrews, this is Miss Carr. She's traveling with us now that she's recovered from her illness." Jenna smiled at Devyn, while sending her the, "please conform with the times" look.

"It's nice to meet you, Mr. Andrews." Devyn had been here long enough now to remember to address men more formally, but it was still a struggle not to use their first names. And she hated when she was spoken to as Miss Carr, but Jenna and Carly had both made it clear she just had to put up with it, unless it was with people she trusted enough to insist they use her given name.

"Well, any time we can add more beautiful ladies to our group is certainly a privilege. So, you're traveling alone then? No husband or family?"

Devyn wasn't quite sure how much to say. They'd all decided to try keeping the story of how she ended up there without much detail.

"It's just me, but I've been lucky to have these families take me in and ensure I get to Oregon safely."

"If I can ever be of any assistance to you, please let me know. I'm traveling with my sister and her husband." He waved his hand toward the heavily pregnant woman walking slowly beside the wagon farther back on the trail. "I'm trying to help as much as I can to ease her burden, but I would be happy to help you in any way too. We're all doing our best to get to the end of our travels safely and can never have too much help."

"Well, thank you very much, Mr. Andrews. I appreciate your offer and will be sure to let you know if I ever need anything." Devyn took in the clean-shaven face and noticed he was actually quite good-looking. His eyes were blue, but not as bright as Luke's. She gave herself a little shake to remember there really wasn't a reason to compare the two men.

Perhaps Mr. Andrews, Esquire, was the man Dr. Lachele sent her here to meet. A lawyer back in these times would certainly be a good, solid choice for a woman.

As her eyes followed the back of the man in the suit walking away, she noticed he did fill it out nicely. He was a man who could offer good looks and seemed to be a nice man. He also had a job that would provide a stable income and that was definitely a plus in her books.

But as she watched, a rider moved into her view and met her gaze. Even from where she stood, she could feel the blueness of his eyes reaching in and holding her.

And if she wasn't mistaken, she could almost swear he didn't look very happy for her to be watching that other man walk away.

CHAPTER 6

"We'll be stopping for the night just up here in a clearing by the river. Then we'll start taking some of the wagons that are ready across tomorrow. Since we're making good time, we can stretch the crossing over a couple of days to allow everyone to rest a bit when we get to the other side."

Luke pulled the reins to sidestep the orange cat that had decided to run past him. Luckily Moe was a good horse and didn't spook easily or he might have ended up on the ground beside the cat.

"Jasper!" Devyn scolded the cat who wasn't paying any attention to her as he chased behind Mary. She looked up at him with eyes as green as emeralds and offered him a smile. "I'm sorry. I really didn't think it through bringing him with me, but I couldn't bear the thought of leaving him behind either. I know he's a bit of a nuisance out here."

The ladies were walking at the back of their wagons, so he'd stopped to tell them the plans after speaking with Hunter and Adam. Normally he would only bother to let the men on each wagon know the plans for the night, but he had decided it wasn't too much trouble to make an extra stop to let the women know too before moving on to the next wagon.

After seeing Stewart Andrews talking to Devyn today, he'd found himself annoyed with every little thing. It had seemed like anything that could go wrong, had gone wrong, so he was ready to stop for the day.

"It's fine. Just keep a close eye on him or he's apt to get stepped on by an animal not as easy to control. You need to be more careful because he could cause an accident or injure one of the live-stock. We can't afford anything like that to happen out here."

His voice was short, and he immediately regretted sounding so angry. Even in the shade of the late afternoon skies, he could see her cheeks redden underneath her bonnet before she looked away.

"I hope you'll join us for the evening meal again tonight, Luke. We'll be sure to put enough out for you."

Luke tipped his head toward Carly. "Thank you. I'll stop by as soon as I've made sure everyone is stopped and secure for the night."

He glanced at Devyn who was avoiding his gaze as she walked alongside her friends. If what they were telling him about where they came from really was true, he had to give her credit for adapting so well to the life on the trail. He knew he hadn't heard her complain once, when there were some women who had lived like this their entire lives who were complaining every single day.

He kicked his heels to guide Moe to the wagon behind, deciding he'd make sure to be extra nice to Devyn when he stopped to eat with them this evening. Although why he even cared if he'd upset her, he didn't understand. Too many hours in the saddle and hot sun had surely addled his brain.

"Luke, here, we saved you some biscuits. And there's more bacon in that pan over by the fire." Minnie met him as he walked into the camp, holding a metal plate out for him. "There's fresh butter on the biscuits, and I'm sure they're still warm."

He smiled down at the older woman who was fussing over his meal. "Thank you, Minnie. I appreciate you ladies taking such good care of me every evening." His eyes took in Jenna and Carly, who were washing dishes at the back of the wagon. He'd been a bit later than usual while tending to the livestock who were getting tired and running low on food. He would be so glad when he got everyone to Oregon, including the poor animals who had made the long journey too.

"Where is Miss Carr? I hope she's faring all right with just being thrown right into things out here. I'm sure it's a challenge for her." He bit into the warm biscuit, savoring the melted butter as it slid down his throat.

"Oh, Devyn is fine. She's always been tough on the outside, so she's adjusting to life on the trail easily enough." Jenna pointed off to the side where he could see Devyn standing with Adam beside their milk cow, Annie. "In fact, she wanted to learn how to do everything she could out here to help, and after I told her how great I did the first time milking Annie, she just had to try it for herself."

He slowly chewed, unsure if he should go over

and help, or just sit back and hope Adam could handle things. As he watched, Devyn sat down on the stool and had milk splattering into the bucket within seconds.

Jenna shook her head and laughed. "Of course, Devyn has always been able to learn things much faster than most people. And it helps that she really doesn't have any fear of anything. She just jumps in with both feet and tries it."

"Well, sometimes that's not a good thing. Like coming here." He looked between Jenna and Carly, who came over to sit on the crates across from him. "Why would you ladies come here, to a time that's not familiar to you? I just don't understand it. From what Hunter and Adam have told me, things are much more advanced and easier in your time. Why would you choose to give that up, to come here?"

Jenna clasped her hands together on her knees as she looked toward the man who was helping Devyn with the milking. "I came here for him."

Carly nodded beside her. "We were sent here to find the men we were meant to be with. And, when you're with someone you love, all that other stuff just doesn't matter."

"But didn't you have loved ones back where you came from? Surely there are people missing you."

The women looked at each other, then glanced at Devyn. "We had no one. The three of us never had families, and we grew up together, with only each other to depend on. Devyn had finally found a brother, and she'd been so happy to have the family she'd always dreamed about. But, from what she's told us, he broke her trust in a terrible way, so she decided to come and be with us. Even if she wasn't coming for a love match, like we did."

He pulled his eyebrows together. "So, she didn't come here to find someone like you ladies did?"

Jenna shrugged, then stood up to get the coffeepot from the hook and poured some into a cup for him. "Doctor Lachele works in strange ways, so we aren't really sure."

He couldn't keep his eyes off Devyn, who was standing up now and laughing with Adam. Her bonnet was hanging off the back of her neck, with her black hair loose around her shoulders. Something about the sound of her laughter caused a stirring in his chest. He had to admit to himself, he was attracted to her, and it would be difficult watching her make a "love match" with someone on the trail, if that's truly what she was here for.

"Is Luke here? I need to find the captain."

He heard Minnie talking to a man who sounded

frantic, so Luke quickly stood to see what the commotion was about. She led Stewart around the corner of the wagon, and Luke instantly felt a twinge of annoyance that the man had come around again.

But he soon realized something was wrong by the lack of color in the other man's face. "What's going on?"

"It's my sister. She's having the baby, but she's not doing well. Something is wrong."

Luke swore under his breath. He knew the woman had been due to have her baby soon, and he'd just hoped everything would go smoothly. He should have known he wouldn't be that lucky.

"Carly, go get Devyn. She can help." Jenna came over and stood next to the men. "Devyn is a midwife. And she's the best one you could ever ask for. She can help your sister."

Luke glanced over as Devyn ran up to join them, not even paying any attention to him at all. "Mr. Andrews, can you take me to your sister?" She looked quickly at Jenna and Carly. "I will need someone to help me with things like wet cloths and other necessities for a birth."

Before either of the women could volunteer, Luke stepped forward. "I can help. I'm the captain of the wagon train, so I should be there if needed."

It wasn't something he needed to do, but he also wasn't going to let her go off with Stewart Andrews, even if it was for something like this.

And it wasn't at all because he was feeling any jealousy. It was simply because he was the captain of the outfit and felt it was his duty.

Even as they made their way quickly back to the other wagon, that's what he continued to convince himself.

CHAPTER 7

"Mr. and Mrs. O'Reilly, this is Miss Carr. She says she can help you with the birth." Stewart helped her up into the back of the wagon, where the couple had cleared a spot for the woman to lie down on some blankets away from the elements outside.

Devyn crawled over to the woman and reached out for her hand. "Don't worry, Mrs. O'Reilly. I'm a trained midwife and I've helped deliver hundreds of babies." She didn't mention that she'd also had the option for much more advanced medical tools and care at her disposal than she had out here. But women had been birthing babies for thousands of years and nothing much changed in that respect.

She just might have to improvise a bit out here on the trail in the middle of nowhere.

Mrs. O'Reilly gripped her hand tightly, her eyes wide with fear. Sweat dripped from her forehead, her hair hanging limply around her face. "Please, help me. I just know something is wrong."

The husband was tightly gripping her other hand, a large, burly man who looked like he was a child as he watched his wife suffer. "Mr. O'Reilly, I can manage here if you would like to go out and help Mr. Bryan to get some water boiling for me. And I will need some rags, if you can round some up." She had a feeling the poor man wasn't going to be much help in this cramped space, so it would be better if he was doing something he felt was useful. "When it's time for the baby to come, I can get you."

The man looked down at his wife. "Will you be all right? Do you want me to stay?"

She shook her head and offered a weak smile. "I'll be fine now. Miss Carr will take care of me."

After he'd crawled from the wagon, Devyn started her assessment.

"Please, help me deliver this baby safely, Miss Carr. I can't lose another baby. Even if you can't save me, please, save this baby for Mick."

Devyn's heart lurched at the pain in the woman's voice. Sometimes it was easy to forget how much harder things were out here, and how often things went wrong for women having babies. But even though Devyn might not have the medical technology with her, she had the knowledge and skill to make sure she saved both mother and baby.

She wasn't going to let them down.

"You can call me Devyn. And I don't want you to worry. I need you to trust me, okay?" She looked into the other woman's eyes, knowing she was going to need her to be strong for the birth ahead. Dealing with a frantic woman made things much harder.

Mrs. O'Reilly nodded, her eyes still wide in her pale face. "Eliza. And I will. It's just that I had a baby before, but he didn't survive the birth. It hurt poor Mick terribly, and I can't do that to him again."

The woman didn't say anything about the pain Devyn knew she would have been feeling too. It was obvious she had so much love for her husband, she had ignored her own heartache. But Devyn suspected the pleas were for herself as much as her husband.

As she checked Eliza over, she understood what was causing so much difficulty, and could possibly explain what had happened during her first birth too.

Luke came to the back of the wagon, pulling the canvas back and setting a pot inside. "I've boiled some water for you."

As Devyn crawled over to take it, he looked over her shoulder. "How is she doing?"

Devyn reached out to take the rags from his hands, before reaching into the scorching hot water to sterilize her hands. "The baby is breech."

Luke looked at her without moving, so she wondered if he didn't understand what that meant.

"It means, the baby is coming backward. It makes the birth very difficult and dangerous."

He still stood there, expressionless and unmoving. But, before she could explain anything more, she realized both Stewart and Mick were standing just behind him.

"I knew something bad was going to happen again. You've brought her nothing but heartache and pain since the day you married her. She deserved so much more than some farmer who can't give her anything. And now, she's in there suffering, trying to give birth to another one of your babies that could kill her."

A cloud crossed Luke's face and he grabbed Mr.

Andrews by the collar. "Don't you dare speak to this man like that. I know you're worried for your sister, but I will not let you spew hatred to the man who obviously loves her a great deal. This is not the time or place for you to air your displeasure over her marriage choices."

Devyn smiled warmly at Mick while Luke took care of Mr. Andrews. "She will be fine. I've handled breech births before."

Of course, many times that was when the woman would then be taken for a C-section in a modern hospital facility. That wasn't an option out here.

But there had been a few instances where the woman had outright refused the hospital or it had been too late in the labor to have a C-section as an option, and Devyn had safely delivered all of those babies.

So, she just hoped she could manage it out here with the limited resources she had. It was going to be hard on Eliza, but Devyn was going to pray hard that she would have a guiding hand with her as she tried to bring this baby into the world safely.

She pulled the canvas over the opening, not letting herself get distracted by the men arguing outside. She had never seen Luke as angry as he'd been when he'd grabbed the other man, but she was grateful he'd been there to handle it. Poor Mick didn't need any extra burden added to his shoulders right now, and if anything happened to either Eliza or the baby, she was going to need Luke here to help diffuse any problems between the men.

Rolling her sleeves up, she quickly went back to Eliza who was moaning in agony, her head rolling side to side as she tried to find comfort. "If anything happens to me, please don't let Stewart blame Mick for anything. I love my husband, and my family just don't understand. I would follow him to the ends of the earth, and I trust him to always take care of me. None of this is his fault."

Devyn smiled warmly at Eliza. "Don't worry about any of that. You're going to be fine, so you can tell him yourself how much you love him once this is all over, okay?"

Just then, a contraction overtook her small body, and a scream erupted from her throat, breaking into the quiet of the night air that had settled around the camp.

She let Eliza grip her hand tightly, ignoring the pain caused by the woman's surprising strength.

If there was no other reason for Dr. Lachele to have sent her here, Devyn would take this. She had sworn an oath to help women who needed her, and right now, she was Eliza's only hope.

It was going to take everything Devyn had to bring this baby into the world, but she'd also decided there was nothing she wouldn't do to make that happen.

CHAPTER 8

Luke sat quietly with Mick, the crackling of the fire the only sound between them. He knew the man needed to be alone with his thoughts, and every time they heard Eliza scream in pain from inside the wagon, the man would stand up and pace before returning to rest his head in his hands.

Other women, awakened by the screams had come to help but had slowly drifted away when it became clear they couldn't offer much more than Devyn already was.

"Stewart is right. I shouldn't have made her come on this journey. Not in her condition. She's already lost one baby and almost died herself during the birth. I selfishly wanted a child so bad I didn't think of the risks she would face again." Mick didn't even look up as he spoke.

Stewart, thankfully, had turned in for the night. He had his own wagon and was sleeping in it, as he had done every night on the trail. He said he refused to sleep outside, and since he'd only come along to make sure his sister was looked after, he was not going to give up the luxury of at least having something over his head.

"You can't blame yourself for something you have no control over."

Luke almost laughed out loud at the words he was saying. It was the exact same thing he'd done himself for years, but he'd heard so many people saying those words to him, they'd become a belief he couldn't let go of. The fact he didn't really believe them in his own situation was irrelevant. He needed to offer some kind of comfort to the other man.

Another scream tore from the wagon, and this time Mick raced over to the back, then stood there helplessly, unsure what to do. Luke went over to stand with him, but before he could say anything, another cry broke through the night air.

A loud, healthy cry that brought tears to Mick's eyes.

And a cheer went up through the wagon circle.

Luke grinned and slapped the man hard on the back just as the canvas opened, and Devyn smiled down at the new father, holding out a wiggling body wrapped in a warm blanket.

"It's a girl," Devyn called out. Another cheer and congratulations rang out from those who were still awake and waiting for news. "She's a stubborn little fighter who was determined to make an entrance into the world in her own way."

Devyn looked exhausted, her own hair now hanging limply around her face showing the strenuous task she'd just been through. But she had a determined look in her eyes that showed him she would never have let anything happen to that baby.

Mick took the bundle from her, a grin covering his face as he took in his new daughter. Suddenly, he lifted his worried eyes to Devyn. "Eliza…?"

But Devyn smiled reassuringly. "She's tired. But she's a fighter too, and once I've got her cleaned up a bit, you can come in and see her."

Luke didn't say anything to the man about the possibility of something still happening to Eliza. His own wife had lost so much blood during the birth she'd been gone soon after the baby.

Hopefully, Devyn would be able to make sure that wasn't going to happen out here.

The men stood outside waiting for the couple to be reunited, and Luke watched in envy as Mick got to meet his new baby. It was a feeling he hated, because he was truly happy for the man.

But the sting of unfairness was always there.

When Devyn stepped out of the wagon, he offered his hand to help her down. Mick quickly hugged her, thanking her with tears running down his face.

"She's waiting for you. And, if you need me at all through the night, please don't hesitate to come and get me. I will stay awake for a bit anyway. And it looks like some of the other women are here to help as well, so don't be afraid to ask for help." Devyn laughed softly as she accepted the man's joyous appreciation.

Mick climbed up with the bundle in his arms, eager to be back with his wife to enjoy their new family.

As they started walking back to their own site, the cool night air wrapped around them. Nearly everyone else had fallen back asleep for the night, knowing they were starting the river crossing tomorrow. Darkness was broken only by the brightness of the moon and the soft glow from the fire ahead someone had kept going for them next to the wagons.

"You did a good job back there. I was worried things weren't going to turn out favorably when you said the baby was coming breech."

Devyn turned to look at him, a tiredness in her eyes as she pushed a strand of hair back from her face. "I wasn't even sure if you knew what I meant about that. But yes, it can be dangerous for a baby to be born that way."

He looked forward as they walked carefully across the opening between the circled wagons. "That's how my wife died."

He didn't know why he was so open and blunt about it when he'd barely spoken of it to anyone since the day it happened. But he'd sensed a genuineness in Devyn that made him want to confide in her.

She stopped and turned, placing her hand on his arm. "Oh, Luke. I'm so sorry. You'd mentioned losing your wife, but I didn't realize it was during childbirth. This must have been so hard for you tonight."

He shrugged, pulling his arm back and pushing

his hands into his pockets as he looked past her shoulder. "My baby didn't survive the birth and then soon after, my wife was gone too. Nothing anyone could do."

"No, sometimes these things are taken out of our hands and no matter what we try to do, we can't help or fix them."

"When I heard Stewart yelling at Mick about it being his fault, it brought everything back to me. I heard the exact same thing from my father-in-law, except in my case, he was right. I'd made the decision to take my wife from the city where she'd grown up, back out to the country, so I could take over the farm after my pa died. We were far away from any kind of amenities, and she didn't do well with it. I was ready to sell the farm and move her back where she would be more comfortable, but by then it was too late anyway."

"Surely you don't believe it was your fault for moving out into the country? That's absurd. There is no guarantee she would have survived even if she'd been near doctors and medical care. You can't blame yourself for that."

Luke laughed harshly. "Oh, I can. And I have for the past three years. Do you have any idea how it feels watching the woman you swore to love and protect, die because she was giving birth to a child she never even wanted?"

Devyn gasped. "Why would you say she didn't want the baby?"

"She'd told me repeatedly since the day she realized she was pregnant that she wasn't able to look after a child. Especially not out in the middle of nowhere with no one to help her. She'd been raised with nannies and helpers, so being out in a small, dingy wood cabin with none of the amenities she'd grown up with was too much for her to live with. She was so angry with me the entire pregnancy, so I'd finally given in and told her we would move back to the city after the baby was born."

"Oh, Luke. I'm so sorry. I'm sure she would have grown to love the baby. You can't blame yourself for something that was so out of your control."

He turned and started walking again, not sure how to reply. Devyn couldn't understand how fragile Josephine had been. She had never been able to handle the things many women did, but Luke had never faulted her for that. It was how she'd been raised, and they'd both been blinded by their budding love, so they had been unwilling to see the truth.

Luke had no doubt now Josephine wouldn't have

ever become a motherly figure. Her own mother had barely been around, letting her children be raised by a nanny. But back then, when he'd found out she was pregnant, he'd been so hopeful she would find a way to love a child and give him the family he desperately wanted.

It hadn't been fair of him to expect that, and because of it, Josephine had died giving birth to a child she didn't want. It's not something Devyn would be able to understand.

"Well, we all make choices we have to live with. If I could go back, I would never take her away from the city. And, if she'd become pregnant, at least she would have had medical care for a birth that was troublesome. She might have lived, even if the baby didn't."

Devyn kept pace beside him. "You need to stop thinking you're responsible, Luke. Seriously, women can think for themselves you know. I'm sure your wife wouldn't blame you."

He stopped by the low, flickering fire next to Devyn's bedroll and looked out into the darkness. "Yes, she did. Those were the last words she ever said to me."

He walked away, not wanting to see the pity or

sadness in Devyn's eyes. He'd never told anyone what Josephine had said to him as she'd laid on the bed where she'd given birth, but they were words he would take with him to the grave.

CHAPTER 9

"I don't know how I could ever thank you enough. We're both so grateful you were here on this wagon train with us. You were like a gift from God, and we can't even let ourselves think about what would have happened if not for you."

Devyn smiled down at the small baby wrapped in the blanket in her arms before looking up at the parents.

"You don't need to thank me, Eliza. You did the hard part." They shared a laugh as the woman came closer and pulled the blanket down a bit to show more of the baby's face.

"Well, we wanted to thank you, and introduce you to Margaret Devyn O'Reilly."

Devyn opened her mouth but couldn't find any words.

"We've never heard the name Devyn before, so it will be a fine name for our little girl to carry with her to always remember the strong woman who helped bring her into this world." Mick stepped up beside his wife, putting his arm around her shoulders lovingly.

"I think it's a wonderful name. Thank you. I'm truly honored."

Stewart stood behind the couple but moved forward as she handed the baby back to Eliza. "She's a beautiful child. We can only hope she grows up to be as stunning as her namesake." He offered Devyn a smile, but she wasn't feeling as warm toward him as she had previously. After the outburst at the back of the wagon, she wasn't sure he was someone she wanted to spend much time with.

"And I would like to apologize for my behavior last night. I was worried for my sister, and I'm afraid I may have acted in a manner which isn't in my true nature."

She raised an eyebrow and looked toward Mick. "I don't really think I'm the one you need to apologize to."

He sheepishly held his hat between his hands and

nodded. "I've given my apologies to both Mick and my sister this morning. My words weren't appropriate, and I shouldn't have said them."

Luke had walked up beside Devyn, hearing the exchange between everyone. He didn't say anything to Stewart but nodded his head in Eliza's direction. "I hope you're feeling well today, Mrs. O'Reilly. Your daughter is a welcome addition to this weary group of travelers."

Devyn noticed a hard stare pass between Luke and Stewart before he turned back to take the coffee being offered by Jenna. "We're going to start taking the first wagons across within the hour. Mrs. O'Reilly, Mick, we'll let you have a day to rest before taking you over. And we'll leave this group as well, in case you have need of Devyn over the next few hours."

Hunter walked over and leaned against the wagon by Luke. "Adam and I will offer our help with the wagons crossing while the women spend the day washing some clothes down at the river."

"All the help we can get will be appreciated. There are a few wagons I'm nervous about getting across. But the local tribes are set up with the pullies and have done this many times before, so hopefully we can get to the other side without much incident."

He turned to Stewart. "We have extra horses if you'd like to help."

Stewart shook his head. "I'm going to stay back with the remaining wagons in case I'm needed around here."

Devyn wasn't sure what he thought he'd be needed for, when most of the men were helping with the crossing. And the women would be catching up with washing clothes and other tasks they hadn't been able to do during the days on the trail.

"Suit yourself." Luke pushed himself off the wagon he'd been leaning on and started to walk away. "Just remember, tomorrow when it's your turn to go across, you might not have anyone willing to help you."

"Well, Mr. Bryan, need I remind you that you're the captain of the wagon train, and it's your duty to help everyone get across? I'm a lawyer, so I assure you, I know my rights."

Luke stopped and turned slowly, and Devyn worried he was about to grab the other man around the collar again. She stepped in and put her hand onto Stewart's arm, hoping to lead him away. "It will be fine, Mr. Bryan. We can use Mr. Andrews assistance with carrying our clothing to the river and to do some of the other jobs that require heavy lifting around the camp."

She hadn't thought Luke's eyes could go as dark as they were at this moment, but he finally just turned and walked away with Hunter and Adam beside him.

"That man needs to learn to control his temper. Honestly, as leader of this wagon train, he needs to remember what his job is."

"I believe Mr. Bryan is doing a wonderful job of leading this outfit to Oregon. And, until recently, I don't remember hearing any complaints coming from you." Jenna had walked over next to them, and Devyn almost burst out laughing at the redness of her friend's cheeks, showing her barely controlled anger.

Stewart's eyes widened, and he quickly looked back and forth between Jenna and Devyn. "Oh, goodness. I'm sorry if I've said anything out of turn again. I'm afraid the worry over my sister yesterday, and then my lack of sleep has left me saying things I wouldn't normally utter. I never intended to offend anyone. My deepest apologies."

Devyn didn't think it was worth mentioning the fact that Eliza, Mick or herself had endured a much more stressful night, and had even less sleep than him, but none of them were using that as an excuse for rude behavior.

But she decided to give him the benefit of the doubt. He did truly seem apologetic and maybe he was someone who just spoke without thinking things through. Although she wondered at his skills as a lawyer if this were the case.

"We will gather some of our clothing up to wash if you would like to come back within the hour to help us carry them to the river. Eliza, if you have anything you'd like washed, send them with Mr. Andrews. You need to spend the day resting and looking after that sweet baby."

After the others had left, Devyn sat down with Jenna and Carly to drink a cup of coffee before heading to the river. She was tired and needed all the caffeine she could find to make it through this day.

Jasper came around the side of the wagon, with Gordon and Mary right behind. The cat jumped up on her lap, and she took a moment to enjoy the affection she was giving him.

"How is Jasper going to get across the river, Miss Carr?" Mary sat down beside her and reached her hand out to pat his head.

"Please, I know it's unusual, but I would like you to call me Devyn. I'm not used to being called Miss

Carr where I come from." She smiled warmly at Mary, who was looking at Jasper with worried eyes. "As for Jasper, I'm a bit worried too. He doesn't like water, and I don't know how easy it will be to keep him in a wagon that's being jostled about. We will have to put our heads together and see if we can come up with an idea."

Mary nodded seriously. "I think Mr. Bryan will be able to figure something out. He's been good at getting us across the other times we had to go over a river. But he's never had to worry about a cat before."

Jenna laughed and shook her head. "No, not a cat. But there has been a cow, and a crazy woman who jumped in after the cow." They all laughed as Jenna retold the story of the crossing where she'd been sure her new cow friend, Annie, was being pulled under, so had tried to save her.

"And I was scared that first time going across the river, but I'm not so scared anymore. So, if you need someone to hold your hand tomorrow when you go across for the first time, Devyn, you can sit in the wagon with me. Maybe Jasper will stay there if you're there."

"I would like that, if you would hold my hand. I admit I'm a bit nervous. But I'm glad you have all done it a few times, so can be sure to keep me calm."

Devyn was trying not to let herself worry about what was happening tomorrow, but she'd read enough stories to know these river crossings were dangerous. And the Snake River was one of the worst.

As they sat and enjoyed their coffee, the sounds of the first wagons going into the water reached them. They could hear men shouting orders and horses splashing in the water as they worked together to make sure everyone made it to the other side.

Her heart lurched as her gaze found Luke helping to ease a wagon hooked up to the pully into the water. It was obvious this wasn't his first time, and his horse was well trained under him, but that didn't ease all her worry.

She would be glad when tomorrow night got here, and they were all safely on the other side of the riverbank. Until then, she'd try not to let herself worry about what could happen.

There wasn't a lot that Devyn was afraid of, but this had her feeling uneasy. So, she let herself believe that Mary was right, and Luke was going to be as good as she said at getting them across.

"Thank you for your help carrying everything down to the river for us. It will all be much heavier walking back to the wagons when everything is soaked, so we'll be glad for the extra arms." Devyn smiled over at the man who was crouched beside her wringing out his own items in the cold water. He was the only man doing his own laundry, and seemed to know what he was doing. It made her see him in a much more favorable light. For a man back in this time willing to do "women's work," it was definitely not usual.

She hoped she was doing everything right and had been closely watching how Jenna and Carly did their own laundry, so it wasn't too obvious she didn't have a clue about what she was doing.

"Well, I hope you can see past my less than perfect behavior you've witnessed in the past few hours and see I'm not as horrible as you must be imagining."

Devyn laughed as she scrubbed at the skirt she held under the water. "I don't think you're a horrible person. Sometimes fear and worry can make us act differently than we normally would. I've seen enough from worried husbands and family members during a birth to know it can be difficult to control how we're feeling."

"Yes, I've been quite worried about my sister. She's already lost one baby, and I know it would have been devastating for her to lose another. And I admit I was worried for her own safety as well. It's just her and I now, so I feel a sense of obligation to look after her. I am finding it difficult to let go and believe her husband can look after her, I suppose. Although I do wish she'd found someone who could have provided a more stable life and income, but I guess I will have to accept what is."

"Eliza is lucky to have a brother like you to look out for her. I'm sure she appreciates it." Devyn kept her eyes on the clear water along the bank as she continued to scrub. She had hoped for the kind of relationship with her brother that was obvious between Stewart and Eliza. But things were different back in this time, and she thought maybe families must take their sense of obligation more seriously.

Plus, Eliza and Stewart had grown up together, so they had formed a bond, whereas she and Darryl had only met recently. There had never been any kind of bond between them, and what she was hoping for wasn't as important to her brother. At least, not as important as the lifestyle he'd fallen into.

Her gaze was drawn downstream to where the wagons were making their way across. There were already quite a few safely settled on the far bank, and she was grateful for the men who were out working so hard to get everyone through the swirling water without too much trouble. The local native tribes had a good system set up here to make things easier, and she was glad to have the chance to witness it.

She'd heard a few of the travelers expressing their fear at seeing the "Indians," and she wished she could explain to the others everything she'd learned about them from reading the history books. These tribes helped the white travelers and were no threat whatsoever. They would receive payment for their help and were a vital part of helping settlers moving west.

As she watched, Luke was on Moe, riding alongside a wagon that was struggling. She could hear the orders being shouted between the men, and she held her breath as the horse lost his footing. Luke managed to keep him under control, all while ensuring the safety of the wagon beside him.

It was obvious he'd done this many times, but there was always danger involved in a crossing like this. But she had to admit, she felt a whole lot safer knowing Luke would be beside them when it was their turn tomorrow.

"If you'll allow me, I can help you ladies get your baskets back up to the wagon." Stewart smiled warmly at Jenna and Carly too. He'd spent the morning at the river helping every way he could, trying to win both of her friends over. Devyn thought Carly might be seeing him in a better light, but she wasn't sure Jenna was so easily swayed.

Devyn wasn't going to let it bother her. She'd seen a good side of Stewart and was willing to give him a chance.

He loaded the heavier ones in his arms, leaving them to only have the lighter items to bring up. As they walked back to the wagons, Devyn noticed the man beneath the suit. He was obviously a kind man who cared a lot about family, and he'd truly made their work easier today by being around.

He was trying, and sometimes that was what mattered the most.

～

"Minnie, I have to tell you again. No one makes biscuits quite like you do." Luke smiled warmly at the older woman as she blushed over his compliment.

"Young man, I know you're just saying that because you're hungry. But thank you."

He took another bite, then lifted a piece of bacon to his mouth. He was so grateful these families always provided him with meals after a day on the trail, and today it was especially appreciated. They had managed to get the majority of the wagons across, leaving only a few for tomorrow. So, they'd be able to spend the rest of the day relaxing a bit before heading out on the trail again.

It had been a grueling day, and he might not have pushed so hard to get as many across as he had, if not for the fact, every time he'd looked back at camp, he'd seen Stewart hanging around Devyn. He didn't trust the man, and he didn't like the thought of him taking advantage of her as a single woman on the trail.

He'd had found himself feeling such annoyance over it, and had kept working harder to not let himself think too much about why it was bothering him.

At least, for now, the man seemed to have gone back to his own camp, leaving Devyn alone.

"How will we get Jasper across, Mr. Bryan?"

Mary had come over and sat on a crate beside him, looking up at him with concern in her eyes.

"Miss Carr...I mean, Devyn, is really worried about him. He's scared of water, and I don't think kitties are very good swimmers. What if he falls in the water?"

Luke suspected the little girl was actually more worried than Devyn by the way she was looking at him for answers. But he lifted his gaze to find Devyn watching him, and saw she was listening closely for his answer.

"Well, I hadn't really thought about it. I don't imagine he will stay in the wagon when it's being lurched across the water, will he?" He smiled down at Mary. "But, for the time it takes to get him across the water, we could put him inside a crate, so he can't get out."

Mary's eyes opened wide, and she shook her head. "But he will be so scared. And besides, I've seen lots of times when crates have fallen out of the wagons and broken open or got lost going down the river. He would be stuck."

Luke couldn't believe he was actually sitting here trying to figure out how to get a cat across a river. It was absurd, and he had more important things to worry about, like the safety of the people and all the livestock in his care. But he also didn't want to see Mary or Devyn worried, even if it was just over a silly cat.

"I'm sure he will be fine, Mary." Devyn reached across and squeezed Mary's hand, giving her a reassuring smile. "We can stay in the wagon with his crate and make sure he's safe. Remember, you promised to stay with me and hold my hand for this crossing to make sure I'm not scared."

Something about her eyes told him Devyn was putting on a braver face than she was feeling. He honestly didn't think she would be afraid of anything, but he was determined to get her across and show her he wouldn't let anything happen to her cat.

Or, to her for that matter.

CHAPTER 11

"Just hold the lid tightly closed because if that thing gets out, he's going to end up straight in the river. And with the current as strong as it is, he better be a good swimmer if he does."

Luke wanted to take his words back as soon as he said them. He'd been in a bad mood all morning, ever since Stewart had ended up at their camp as soon as breakfast was finished. He'd offered to have Devyn go across in his wagon, but she'd declined, stating she'd be in a wagon with Mary and Jasper as she'd promised.

Stewart had looked a bit put out but had quickly covered his feelings with a gracious smile. Luke had noticed, though, and it had grated on his nerves at the forwardness of the man to have even made the offer in the first place.

Devyn stood nervously at the back of Hunter's wagon where she was going to ride across with Mary and Carly, and of course, Jasper. The girl was already up in the wagon, settling into a spot right beside the crate they'd closed the cat into. Already, the animal was howling to let his displeasure be known to everyone within a ten-mile radius.

"I'm only joking, Devyn. The crate lid will hold during the crossing. Jasper will be safely locked up in there, and while he might be quite annoyed with you at the other side, I assure you he will get across without a bit of dampness to his paws. I give you my word, if he does get out, I will pull him from the river myself."

She smiled at him and rolled her eyes. "Well, I'm glad to see that chivalry is alive and well in these times."

His chest tightened at the beauty of her face when she smiled. Her dark hair peeked out around the edges of her bonnet, and he had a sudden urge to reach out and see if it was as soft as it looked.

Swallowing hard, he put his hand out to help her up into the wagon. "Just stay put in the wagon, and even if it sounds like it's being ripped apart, I assure you, we have things under control out here."

When her fingers clasped his, he had to remind himself to breathe. She held her skirt up with her other hand as she crawled up into the back. For a woman who was physically so petite and dainty, he was still in awe of how well she handled herself out here. Not to mention the night she'd managed to deliver a baby who most likely wouldn't have survived without her.

Devyn was nothing like the sort of woman he had been drawn to in the past. Josephine had been delicate and tall, with hair as golden as the sun. She was the woman he'd always dreamed of falling in love with. And since she had been gone, there wasn't anyone in the world Luke had even found himself looking at.

Until Devyn. He'd have to be blind not to notice her beauty, even if it wasn't the kind which normally turned his head.

Hunter helped Carly up and he leaned in to kiss her. Luke ignored the lonely ache in his heart as he turned to give them their privacy.

He'd had his chance to be loved but had demanded she try being someone she wasn't. He deserved the loneliness he felt.

Luke mounted his horse and waited for the first wagons to be hooked to the pullies. He had complete faith in the abilities of the men who had done this many times before, so he waited until the wagons started to ease into the water. He could see Devyn sitting in the wagon as it bounced over the first few rocks in the shallow bank, her body swaying as the canvas moved back and forth, letting him see inside.

He wished he could somehow make these crossings a bit easier for everyone, knowing how much of a worry they were. Plus, he was sure being jostled around in the back of a hard wagon, completely at the mercy of the water and men outside helping maneuver them, was hard on the women and children.

Adam's wagon was just ahead of Hunter's, where Jenna and Minnie were riding. The milk cow, Annie was being led across by Adam on his horse, who wasn't taking any more chances of his wife jumping out to save it.

He'd never seen women so attached to animals in his life. Jenna and the cow, then Carly and her dog. He really shouldn't have been surprised when the next girl from the "future" showed up with some animal she relied on for comfort and companionship. The people in their time must be a lot more dependent on animals than what was common for this time period. Luke had only really seen animals as a necessity, either for food or performing a duty, like helping to guard livestock.

He moved his horse as needed, helping to guide the heavy animals pulling the wagons through the deep water. Now and then, Moe would lose his footing, and Luke had to fight to keep him under control. Luckily, his horse was well trained and had done this enough times to keep from getting spooked at the noises and commotion.

The wood of the wagons groaned with the pressure of the water hitting the sides as the wheels bounced over the uneven bottom. They were almost to the halfway point, which was the most difficult part, but once they got past there, the wagons could easily be pulled back up the bank on the other side.

Just when he thought they were at that point, one of the wheels on Hunter's wagon hit a rock hard, shattering the wooden wheel. He quickly turned Moe, trying to get to the wagon that was listing perilously to the side. The men on the pullies started hollering to hurry, wanting to drag it to the bank before more damage could happen.

Luke watched helplessly as the back of the wagon tipped low into the water, and before he could even react, he saw a crate fall out of the back. He heard Devyn's scream at the same time the lid came open and he knew exactly which crate it was.

The mournful wailing of the now drenched cat as he tried to cling to the crate for safety was all he could hear. But he needed to focus on getting Hunter's wagon across with the people inside. He didn't have time to deal with a drowning cat.

As he maneuvered Moe over, his eyes locked on Devyn's, and he knew in that moment, she wasn't going to wait for him to get Jasper. Growling loudly, he turned back to follow the crate that was being dragged downriver. In all his life, he never thought he'd let a woman make him feel obligated with a simple look to save a cat that shouldn't even be out here in the first place.

Just as he caught up to the crate that was swirling dangerously fast in the current, he heard another scream coming from the wagons. He quickly reached down and grabbed the cat by the scruff of the neck, and turned Moe around to see what was happening, just in time to see Devyn go tumbling out of the back.

Fury and fear gripped him as he raced Moe dangerously fast over the slippery rocks on the bottom of the river, raging against the current as they hurried back. He ignored the pain of the cat's claws as they gripped his neck, his eyes only seeing Devyn in the water.

But, as soon as he had reached her, she was standing up and yanking at her skirts to walk the rest of the way. She cried out in joy when she noticed the cat in his arms, but he was too angry to enjoy the moment of being a savior to a now drenched feline.

He reached down and grabbed onto one of her arms, pulling her up onto his lap.

"Luke, what are you doing? I'm perfectly capable of walking the rest of the way now. We're almost at the bank."

"Just hang on, you foolish woman. I'm not in the mood to be risking my horse's, or my own safety to be chasing after you downriver too. What were you thinking? I have better things to be doing than dealing with useless animals that don't belong out here, or women who can't follow simple instructions." His words came out angry as he focused on getting Moe up onto the bank.

As soon as they stopped, the horse's sides heaving from the exertion, Devyn jumped down and faced him, her eyes glaring at him with anger.

"I wasn't thinking anything. I was leaning out to

see if you had got Jasper and fell out. I didn't jump in on purpose just to make your life more difficult. And, I was more than able to walk the rest of the way. The water wasn't that deep anymore, and I've been swimming all my life. I did not need you coming in to grab me and treat me like some spoiled child who had done something wrong."

Jasper jumped out of his arms now, racing away up the bank toward the wagons already set up in the camp. She watched him go, then turned back to Luke.

"Thank you for saving Jasper. I'm aware you had better things to be doing, but I appreciate your help. Now, if you'll excuse me, I'm going to find the *useless* animal that happens to mean a great deal to me. You can get back to doing your more important jobs."

She dismissed him before he could even say a word. What could he say anyway?

He'd acted like a complete oaf, simply because he'd been caught off guard by the terror he'd felt, seeing her fall from the wagon. He knew she was right. They were almost to the bank by that point, and she likely would have been fine walking the rest of the way without incident, but it had scared him.

And it was a feeling he wasn't comfortable with, so he'd reacted badly.

Watching her retreating back, he could see the anger in the way she was holding her shoulders, not even concerned about her soaked skirts as she walked with her head high.

He groaned inwardly and turned Moe back around to focus on bringing the rest of the wagons over. He had a job to do, so he didn't have time to be chasing after an angry woman. When he got back to camp today, he would try talking to her.

But he wasn't sure she was going to even give him the time of day.

CHAPTER 12

Devyn scrubbed her arms with the bodywash, not even caring about the coldness of the water she sat in. Her friends stood with blankets, making a bit of privacy as they'd each taken turns having a bath in the river. She'd kept her underclothes on, not willing to get completely naked out here in the middle of nowhere with so many people milling around from the wagon train.

All the wagons had made it across, and while the men were working to repair the broken wheel on Hunter's wagon, the women had all come down for a wash. Minnie had already taken Mary back up to the wagons, so it was just the three of them left.

"He's just so infuriating! It's not like I did it on purpose, so he could come riding up like my knight in shining armor to save me. And, I know he could have just left Jasper to drown, but honestly, the way he talked to me, he's lucky I didn't pop him across the chin like I wanted to."

Carly and Jenna had their backs to her, but she heard them both laugh clearly.

"I can honestly say if these are the kind of men available here, then I'm beginning to believe Doctor Lachele took me up on my offer of just sending me here to be with my friends again. There's no grand, exciting, true love for me. Not with these choices."

"Well, out of them, Luke is at least the better option, you have to admit." Jenna still hadn't decided she liked Stewart too much, so she obviously would think Luke was a better choice.

"No, I don't have to admit it. He comes and goes, never shows any real interest in me, and then embarrassed me completely in front of everyone within earshot by the riverbank today. Not only that, the one time we actually did have a meaningful conversation, he made it quite clear he was completely in love with his deceased wife, and he intends to never be with anyone else ever again."

She stepped out of the cold water and dried herself as much as possible, then walked over to her friends who moved closer to allow her a sheltered area to change into clean underthings. Thankfully, the late afternoon air was still fairly warm, so she was unlikely to end up with pneumonia, even after two dumps in a freezing cold river in one day.

"Devyn, you have to give him a break. He did save Jasper, after all."

Devyn shot an annoyed look at her friends who were grinning at each other as though they knew some big secret she didn't know.

She hastily put her clothes on, then grabbed her things from the ground and started to make her way back to camp. Her friends fell into step beside her, and they walked along in silence for a few seconds before Carly finally spoke.

"You know, Devyn, I didn't want to admit it at the time, but I knew without a doubt in my heart that Hunter was the man I'd come here for. Even if my mind didn't quite know for sure, when I look back, I always knew deep inside."

Jenna nodded in agreement. "For me, it was hard because I was sure Adam was the one, but he was engaged to another woman. Do you know how difficult it was knowing in my heart he was who I'd come here for, but that somehow Doctor Lachele must have made a mistake?"

Devyn had heard the story before and remembered how heartbroken Jenna had been when she'd briefly come back to their time, sure she'd missed her chance with her true heart match. But everything had worked out for them, and it was because there was no doubt whatsoever, they were made for each other.

"I know, and I'm so happy you both had everything work out so well for you. But I'm different. I really didn't ask to come here for a love match, although I wasn't opposed to one if it happened. But I'm not going to force something that isn't meant to be."

"I'm not saying for sure Luke even is intended for you. I think we all just got hung up on the whole Luke Bryan thing and made it more than it needed to be. You've barely had time to know him much at all. I'm just saying that I've known him for a long time now and he's a good man. He might be a bit intense when it comes to his duties as captain, but deep down he's got a kind heart. I know you're angry with him for today, but are you sure it's not actually more a case of wounded pride?"

Devyn looked at the wagons ahead and saw the people milling around getting the evening meal prepared. While life on the trail was more difficult than anyone in her time could actually imagine, she'd often found herself feeling such a sense of camaraderie and companionship with these fellow travelers, it was something she'd never encountered before. And it gave her a sense of peace that was unfamiliar to her.

"Just keep your mind open to the possibilities, even if that ends up being Stewart." Jenna pretended to shiver in distaste but smiled at her to soften the effect. "And, if it ends up being neither one, then you can just stay with us until you do find him."

As though he heard them talking about him, Stewart appeared just as they got next to the wagons.

"I'm relieved to see you are all right, Miss Carr. I saw you fall in the river as we were getting our wagon lined up to come across and I feared the worst."

Devyn cringed, knowing now that they'd even noticed her humiliation from the other side of the bank too. So, they all would have seen her being manhandled onto the back of a horse and likely even heard her being scolded like a child.

Which meant pretty much every single person in the entire wagon train had witnessed it. Any softening she might have had toward Luke after talking with her friends, came back with a fury.

"I'm fine, Mr. Andrews. And I'm truly happy to have someone show me some concern. It's been a tiring day, and I appreciate seeing a friendly face."

"Well, let me escort you back to your wagon and hopefully we can have some time to visit and relax. I'm glad we managed to get everyone across without too much trouble, other than your incident."

Devyn smiled up at the man and placed her free hand on his arm, while she tucked her wet towel and underthings under the other. She decided she wasn't going to give Luke Bryan, the captain of this wagon train, another thought today. And, if this handsome man beside her was willing to offer her some kindness, she was more than happy to accept it.

As they came around the back of their wagon, she instantly locked eyes with the man she wasn't going to think about. For a brief moment, she thought she'd noticed a smile on his face and perhaps a bit of remorse in his eyes. But that was soon replaced with his usual clouded expression, and he turned and walked away without a word.

And that was completely fine with her.

CHAPTER 13

Luke leaned against his still rolled up bedroll and let his gaze fall on the sleeping figure he could see by the dim, flickering light of the fire by Hunter's wagon. Even from here, he could see the dark hair flowing out onto her pillow.

He hated his fascination with her. And that's all he was willing to admit it was. She was a beautiful woman who had suddenly shown up, making him in charge of her safety. That's all it really came down to.

But even as he told himself that, he was reminded that there were other women on this wagon train who didn't draw his attention like her. Plus, both Jenna and Carly had just shown up like Devyn, and while they were both very stunning women, they hadn't consumed his thoughts like Devyn did.

He knew he owed her an apology and had fully intended to give her one as they'd gathered to eat this evening. But when he'd seen her coming back from the river with Stewart, her cheeks reddened from the coldness of the water while her hair had hung in wet tendrils around her shoulders, it had angered him. All his good intentions of trying to make things right with her had disappeared.

Instead, he'd moped off and spent the remainder of the evening helping with jobs about the camp, not bothering to join them for their meal. He comforted himself with the knowledge that's what he should be doing as captain anyway. He really didn't have time to be soothing over a woman's displeasure with him.

As he watched, the woman he was thinking about turned and threw the blankets off before reaching her hands up to stretch. She sat and stared at the fire for a few moments unmoving as she seemed to be lost in her thoughts. When she lifted her gaze and looked in his direction, he didn't even breathe, scared she would see him sitting in the darkness.

Finally, she turned her head and reached into her bag, taking something out. She looked around before placing her pillow to rest against the wheel of the wagon, then leaned back and put something in her ears.

He finally let go of the breath he'd been holding, transfixed as he watched her. Her head went back, and she closed her eyes, and even though he wasn't close enough to see, he was sure by the way she was holding herself there would be a smile on her face.

What was she thinking about that made her seem so happy, and at peace? The thought that it might be Stewart made his chest lurch with sudden anger.

Standing up quickly, he strode across the open ground between them, determined she was going to hear his apology one way or another. Everyone else in the camp had long since gone to sleep for the night, so at least he wouldn't have to worry about interruption from the other man who was always hanging around.

As he got up closer to her, he realized she hadn't even heard him approach, her head still back against the wagon with her eyes closed. He could hear her softly singing words he didn't recognize. Unsure how to approach, he stood awkwardly staring down at her, not wanting to startle her. He could see something in each of her ears which must not have allowed her to hear his footsteps.

In the light of the dwindling fire, he was

awestruck at how truly beautiful she was. He'd never seen a woman with such perfect features, who didn't seem to even notice her beauty. Most women he'd known used their looks to their advantage, always wanting men to take notice.

But Devyn had never done that. In fact, he'd noticed she really didn't seem to care at all about any of those things. Even now, he noticed she had feet bare poking out from the hem of her skirt. He felt guilty looking, but her ankles were lovely, and even her toes seemed to be perfect.

Suddenly, her eyes fluttered open, and her mouth opened to scream, but she quickly recovered, clamping her hand over the sound. She yanked at the wires that were hanging from her ears and pulled whatever it was out, before reaching down and pushing something she held in her hands among the folds of her skirt.

"Sheesh, Luke, you really shouldn't be sneaking up on women in the dark like that. You're lucky I didn't use some of my self-defense moves on you." Her hand was on her chest now as she breathed heavily. "I thought everyone was sleeping, so was sitting here peacefully enjoying my music."

He stepped over and folded his legs, sitting down

beside her next to the fire. "How are you listening to music?"

She grinned sheepishly and lifted the object out from her skirts. He'd never seen anything like it before. It was small and made of a strange material he'd never seen on the outside. "It's a cell phone. In my time, we used it to call people anywhere in the world, and it also stores our music and pictures and lots of things like that. I brought it with me, along with a solar charger, so I can still enjoy my music until it stops working. And, it's got all my pictures, so I can look back on them too."

He brought his eyebrows together in confusion. "You mean you could call people on that, without any kind of cables or wires, or anything?"

She nodded, then pushed at something on the glass several times before turning it to show him. "This is why we all had a strange reaction when we heard your name the first time. This man is named Luke Bryan too, and he's a famous country music singer. I've always had a crush on him and told everyone he was the only man I would ever marry."

Her mouth suddenly stopped moving, as though she realized she'd said too much, and he watched the redness in her cheeks rise. He lowered his own gaze to look at the thing in her hand and gasped quietly as she handed it to him. He ran his hand over it, and it felt odd to the touch.

"It's called plastic."

He finally looked at the picture. "He looks a lot like me. I've never seen anything like this. And it's in color too." If he'd had any lingering doubt about her coming from the future, it all just disappeared. There simply was no other explanation for what he was looking at here.

She leaned over slightly, and a light floral scent reached his nostrils. He inhaled softly as she slid her finger across the front of the picture and another one came up. This one was a picture of Devyn with barely any clothes on. He could see her shoulders and her legs, and her feet only had some kind of small shoe with just straps holding them on. He tried to look away, knowing it wasn't proper to be seeing a woman like this, but she was looking down at the picture and laughing softly, not in the least uneasy with how she was dressed.

"This was me last summer. It was so hot that day, I look a mess."

His eyes took in the "mess" and couldn't see it the same way she did. He was sure he'd never seen a woman look more stunning and happy. "Are these the kind of clothes you always wear in your time?"

She nodded and slid her finger over the image, showing him another one of her wearing a dress, but it was above her knees and only had little straps, nothing at all like the dresses he was used to seeing cover a woman's body.

"In the summer, women wear clothes that are cooler, like shorts and sundresses. It's unbearable wearing all of these clothes when it's hot, and honestly is one of the hardest things I'm trying to adjust to out here."

He lifted his eyes and saw her looking down at the picture wistfully.

"Do you miss your time? Do you ever think you'd like to go back?" He held his breath as he waited for her answer.

She sat back and looked up at the sky, folding her hands in her skirt in front of her. "I miss a lot of the things that made life easier, and luxuries we just took for granted, like my iced coffees. But there are things here too that are better. It's just taking some time to get used to it all."

She looked around at the wagons and smiled. "I know it sounds strange, because it's so hard out here, but in a way, it's also nice to live a bit simpler."

"You never answered if you ever think about going back."

Her gaze watched the fire flickering in front of them. "I don't really have anything to go back for, so no, I don't think about it."

He'd heard a bit about her brother and how she didn't have any other real family since she'd arrived, and he could tell how much it hurt her. He waited for her to continue, sensing she wanted to talk about it.

"All my life, all I ever wanted was a family, and when I found out I had a brother, I was so happy. To be able to create a bond with someone who shared something together was a dream come true. But, as I got to know him, I realized he wasn't like me at all, and I didn't matter to him as much as I'd hoped." She shrugged, pretending it wasn't a big deal.

"Well, he's the one missing out then. He's a fool for not stepping up to be what a brother should be." He'd never had siblings of his own, and he understood Devyn's desire to have that bond with someone.

He cleared his throat and looked at the picture one more time before handing the object back to her. "I had wanted to come over to apologize for my behavior today. It was rude and I know it's likely hard for you to believe, but I am sorry."

She sighed and smiled up at him. "I was angry

and embarrassed at the time, but I've gotten over it. I know you were just worried and doing your job. Jasper and I both do appreciate your help."

"Still, I shouldn't have spoken to you the way I did. But I'm glad I was able to save your cat for you. I can understand your concern for him. I'd feel the same if it were Moe."

He didn't add that at least Moe was a useful animal, and he had a real reason to feel the bond he did with the animal. As he was finding out, there was a lot about women from their time period that really didn't make sense to him.

He stood up and turned to look down at her. "You should get some sleep. It's going to be an early morning."

The bright smile on her face was an image he knew he would never forget. And it kept him warm as he crawled into his own bedroll for the night, her green eyes the last thing he remembered as he finally drifted off to sleep.

CHAPTER 14

"Those mountains in the distance are a sign we're nearing the end of the journey. I've heard others saying once you can see Mount Hood, it's only a couple of more weeks of traveling before reaching Oregon City." Stewart walked beside his wagon, looking west toward the mountains they could see ahead.

He'd stopped at their camp this morning and asked if she would mind walking along with Eliza today to help her a bit with the baby. Devyn had immediately agreed, feeling guilty she hadn't thought to make the offer herself, knowing how difficult these daily treks had to be on a new mother.

She looked down at the bundle she carried in her

arms, giving Eliza a much needed break. Little Margaret stared up at her in wonder, still so full of innocence and discovery.

"Do you hear that, sweetheart? We're almost there. You'll be able to always tell the story of how you were born on the Oregon Trail. You're a little miracle." She let the baby clasp her fingers around one of her own and smiled as the eyes fluttered shut again.

"I'm still so grateful for you, Devyn. Honestly, I don't know what I was thinking when I agreed to make this trip in my condition, but at the time, I guess I'd figured we would have made it to Oregon by the time the baby came. I just didn't want to disappoint Mick. This has been his dream for quite some time now."

Stewart looked at his sister with a frown. "Well, it was foolish of you both. I would have never allowed my wife to make this trip while carrying my child, not knowing the risks and hardships along the way."

"Stewart, we've been over this so many times. I know you're angry about us making this trip, but we never forced you to come with us. And I make up my own mind. Mick tried to talk me out of it, but I was the one who insisted. So, you need to get over it. If you don't like Mick because you believe he's below our station, whatever you think that might be, then you're going to end up miserable because I've made my choice. I love him and I don't really care what you think."

His eyes clouded over in anger, but he just shook his head and looked away. "I will never believe he's going to be able to give you a good life, but you're right. It's your decision. You've never understood how women should respect the men in their families and abide by their wishes. So someday when you come crying back to me because your husband can't even provide you with enough food to survive, you will be apologizing then."

Devyn pulled her eyebrows together in annoyance, but before she could say anything, Eliza put her arms out to take Margaret, trying to smile at her. She could tell the other woman was fighting back tears. "I'm going to take Margaret and try to lie down a bit in the wagon. I know it's rough but sometimes the rocking helps her to sleep."

Devyn didn't want to point out how the baby was already sleeping quite well in her arms, knowing the woman just needed an excuse to get away from her brother for the moment.

When they were gone, Devyn looked over at Stewart who was scowling ahead. "You know, Mick loves your sister very much, and I don't think it's fair for you to be so hard on her. Aren't you happy she has someone who will care for her as much as he does?"

He shook his head. "No. Mick is a farmer and will never be anything more than that. Nothing against the men who work in the fields and are content to barely survive, but it's no way to take care of a woman or raise children. And Eliza is going to find that out the hard way."

"I don't think that's a fair assumption. This country was built on the backs of those farmers and if not for them, no one else would survive out here without food to eat."

Stewart looked at her and must have realized he'd made her angry, because he quickly changed his expression. "Oh, of course, I understand that. It's just that we were raised in a family who never had to live like that. My father was a lawyer, which is why I became one myself. And my mother lived a pampered life, as Eliza should have too. She will never be pampered living in a hut out in the middle of nowhere, with no money coming in."

Devyn watched him and wondered if he really

was a snob or just horribly uneducated about the life of those farmers on the frontier. It was true they struggled, but many of them raised happy families and lived a life to be proud of.

"Well, sometimes we aren't all dealt a hand as easy as yours. I grew up with nothing, and quite frankly, I believe everything turned out just fine for me."

Perhaps realizing he might have overstepped, he once again changed his expression to look contrite. "Miss Carr, once more I seem to have said something to upset you. I do apologize." The funny thing was, as Devyn listened to his apology, she was hearing the voice of the man who had apologized to her last night at the fire.

Luke's had been heartfelt, and she'd known it the moment he'd spoken. Whereas Stewart's apology seemed forced, as though he was only offering it to get back in her favor—like every other time he'd apologized to her over the past couple of weeks she'd known him.

"Truthfully, I'm not usually such an oaf, however I never wanted to come out west. I was quite happy back home and had all my father's clients to work with. Now, I will be starting over in a place where, to be completely honest, I'm not even sure anyone will have any money to pay me for my services."

"So why did you come then? Your sister would have been fine with her husband."

He looked at her with his eyebrows pulled together in shock. "Because I need to be here when she comes to her senses. She grew up with money and never needing to worry about doing a thing for herself. She's going to be miserable, and I will be the one there saying I told you so. Then, we can turn around and go back home, away from this primitive side of the country."

Devyn's gaze caught the back of the man far ahead as he surveyed the area around them to make sure they were all safe and on solid ground. She remembered the night after Margaret was born when Luke had told her about his own wife, and how he'd taken her away from her pampered life. He still believed he hadn't been good enough for her and shouldn't have taken her from that life.

Hearing another man talk about someone just like him, brought out a sense of protection within her. Who was Stewart to say he knew what was best for someone, and that Mick wasn't good enough for his sister? Because that's what it really came down to. Stewart believed he was beneath their station.

The same way Josephine's family had looked at Luke.

"I have a feeling you're going to be waiting a very long time to hear those words from your sister. She is a strong woman. I witnessed her strength first-hand, and I have also gotten to see just how much her husband loves her. I have no doubt he will do everything in his power to protect her and give her a good life. She does not need you hanging around, making her feel guilty for any choices she's made. I would suggest when you get to Oregon City, you make plans to head back home because your sister will be happily living there with her family."

His mouth dropped open, then quickly clenched shut. He closed his eyes briefly as though he was desperately trying to figure out what to say.

She admitted her words might have come out a bit stronger than she'd intended, but all she could think about was the pain she'd heard in Luke's voice when he'd told her about his wife. No man should ever be made to feel like that. And Stewart was determined to do that to Mick, and to Eliza too.

"If you'll excuse me, Mr. Andrews, now that Eliza has no more need for me here, I think I will go back and join my friends."

She turned and left, without even waiting for him

to reply. Deep down, she did believe Stewart was a good man, but he sure had a knack for saying the wrong things around her.

And today, she wasn't in the mood for listening to any more of his apologies.

CHAPTER 15

"There's nothing quite like an impromptu party to ease some of the burden. I guess everyone is feeling the excitement building from almost being at the destination." Hunter sat on a crate next to Luke, tapping his foot in time with the fiddle music coming from the center of the camp.

"I think the strain of the past few months has taken its toll, and for some people, they're unsure how to feel at this leg of the journey. It's always hard on those who have survived but lost their loved ones along the way, and some are just so weary they're questioning whether coming was the right thing to do. I'm glad they can let themselves enjoy things a bit tonight, sharing in some fun with the people who have been part of their lives for so many weeks before they part ways."

He'd seen this happen before and understood the mixed feelings everyone was experiencing. They were all excited to get to Oregon and start their new lives, but for some, with all the losses they'd experienced along the way, their dreams had already been shattered. Some were just so tired at this point; they had lost their excitement for their future.

But for all of them, they knew soon they'd be going on to whatever new beginnings they were destined for and would be saying goodbye to a lot of people who had become like family along the way.

He knew it would be hard for him to say his farewells to Hunter and Adam, and their families. They'd welcomed him in more than any other group he'd met on other trips west, and he was grateful to have met them. It really was a feeling he wasn't used to.

Devyn came over and sat down across from him while Carly and Jenna sat next to their husbands, leaning into their shoulders. Mary walked over and sat up on Hunter's knee. "Did you help the women with the dishes, Mary?"

"Yes, I did. But I dropped a plate on the ground,

and then Devyn had to rewash it, but she wasn't mad. She laughed."

Devyn grinned over at Mary. "Why would I get mad over a dropped plate? Besides, you've done such a good job looking after Jasper for me all this way, I could never be mad at you."

"I wish Jasper could come live with me. I'm sure going to miss him." Mary rested her head against Hunter's shoulder.

"Well, you can always visit him."

"But aren't you staying in Oregon City? I thought Carly said you weren't sure what you wanted to do when you got there, but you'd likely stay there for the winter until you decided."

Devyn's gaze turned toward the couples who were starting to dance on the dusty ground between all the wagons. "I'm not sure, that's true. But hopefully by the time we get there, I'll have decided. I don't want to just be tagging along all the time, so I don't really know." She shrugged her shoulders and looked down, but he could see the redness of her cheeks.

"Devyn Carr, I've told you a million times you're not tagging along if you join us as we go to Bethany. We want you to come. That's the whole reason you came here, wasn't it? To be with your friends. And just because we're now both married, it doesn't mean we don't have room for you in our lives anymore." Jenna stood up and reached out to take her hand. "Now come on. We're all going to go out and have some fun dancing and visiting with the others. This is a perfect night to let ourselves relax a bit."

Luke slowly stood too, walking slightly behind everyone else as they made their way over to mingle with the others. Another fiddle had come out, along with someone playing the harmonica. He heard laughter as they approached, and he hoped Devyn could have some fun tonight. He'd seen the worry in her eyes, and a touch of sadness too over thoughts of her future out here.

Mary was skipping with excitement, with Gordon and Jasper right on her heels, getting under everyone's feet. But the others were all quite used to the trio and didn't seem to mind. They found a few of the other children in the outfit, and they all chased each other around, enjoying the chance to just be kids for a short time.

Hunter quickly pulled Carly out for a dance as an upbeat song started, and Adam and Jenna were right behind. An older gentleman came over to offer his hand out to Minnie, leaving Luke alone with Devyn for the first time since they'd sat by the fire a couple of nights ago.

He put his hand out to her and shrugged, grinning down at the look of disbelief on her face. "What? Don't you think I can dance?"

She threw her head back and laughed, shaking her head as she took his hand. "No, I actually didn't think you would be much of a dancer. But, truthfully, it's me you need to worry about. I don't have a clue how to dance like this, not to mention the extra fifty pounds in skirts I'll have to try maneuvering with."

"Well, I guess you'll just have to follow my lead, and try not to get your feet in my way."

His chest clenched with joy at seeing her laughter, and as he put his arm around her waist and pulled her into his arms for the dance, he had a moment of worry for his sanity. Being this close to her was dangerous, but he couldn't just leave her standing there with no one to dance with.

So, he was willing to make the sacrifice and risk making a fool of himself if it gave her a few moments of happiness.

Her face was covered with a smile as she looked up at him. Those green eyes that had kept him awake many nights since meeting her, sparkled with laughter as she let him spin her around in his arms.

"I don't know what I'm even supposed to be doing with my feet. I'm going to end up spraining an ankle." Her breath touched the skin of his neck, sending tingles down his spine.

"You're doing fine. Just hold onto me, and I'll keep you safe." As he said the words, her smile faltered, and he wondered what she was thinking.

But she nodded and held on. "You've done a good job so far."

As they spun on the uneven ground beneath them, he couldn't take his eyes off her. It felt like they were the only ones there, and he knew he was getting himself in too deep. But he just couldn't make himself stop, not wanting to let her go.

Finally, a break in the music forced them apart, and she looked up at him with red cheeks and a bright smile. "Thank you for that. I truly needed some fun."

He pulled on the tip of his hat; sure his own grin was even wider. "Glad to be at your service, ma'am."

They started to walk over to where the others had gathered, but before they made it back, Stewart came along and put his hand out for hers. "Miss Carr, I hope you'll allow me a turn."

Luke thought a displeased look momentarily crossed her face, but then she graciously smiled and took his offered hand. He wanted to grab her arm and refuse to let her go with the other man, but he knew he was being ridiculous. Even Jenna and Carly were now taking a turn with other men while their husbands danced with some of the other ladies.

It's not like Luke had any right to demand Devyn only dance with him.

He hoped the annoyance he was feeling wasn't showing on his face as he walked over and put his hand out to Minnie. The last thing he was going to do was sit around sulking like a jealous suitor.

So he ignored the rising anger he felt every time he spun around with Minnie and saw Devyn in another man's arms.

She was simply a woman in his care until they got to Oregon City. He was responsible for her safety, and that was it.

And he would continue to tell himself that repeatedly until he believed it himself.

CHAPTER 16

Devyn folded her knees and tucked her feet in close, hugging her arms around them as she leaned back and looked up at the sky. The sound of the fiddles and laughter reached her ears from a distance, and she smiled to herself, glad to have had the chance to enjoy herself so much this evening.

After dancing a few times, though, she'd found her way back to the wagon to just be alone with her thoughts for a while. The past few days had filled her with so many mixed emotions and she was having trouble figuring it all out herself.

She was so happy being back with her friends again, but the closer they got to Oregon, the more she was second guessing her decisions. She was truly happy for her friends, but they had new lives now with husbands and families, so while she tried not to feel like a third-wheel, the feeling had stirred now and then.

Everything had changed so much from when they were younger and only needed each other to be happy. And, Devyn was going to have to accept that as they all grew and found new paths in life.

Then, there was the whole thing she was dealing with as far as Luke was concerned. She couldn't deny the feelings she had for him anymore, even though she knew he could never reciprocate them. Why would Dr. Lachele have sent her to a man who wasn't ready to fall in love?

"I wondered where you'd gone off to. Mind if I join you for a bit? I don't know if my feet can take much more dancing."

Devyn jumped as the man she'd been thinking about came around the side of the wagon and sat down beside her. She looked back up at the sky, not wanting to let herself feel the closeness of him.

"Is everything all right? I noticed you seemed a bit melancholy tonight, so was worried when I didn't see you out dancing anymore."

She smiled and pulled her knees in closer. "I'm

okay. I just needed a bit of a break from everything, so came to look up at the stars. It's always so amazing to me how they are so bright and seem to stretch on forever. These same stars are the ones I would have been seeing in my own time, although living around New York didn't let me see them like this."

She could sense his gaze on her for a moment before he leaned back and looked up too. "It's humbling when you see how small you are compared to everything out there. I've always loved the night sky. Seems to make it easier to work through your thoughts."

They sat in silence for a while, enjoying the sounds of the fiddle and people having fun behind them, away from the darkness where they sat.

"Mary mentioned you weren't sure what you're doing when we get to Oregon City. I thought you'd planned to go on with your friends to where they'll be settling."

She shrugged and rested her chin on her upturned knees. She figured this likely wasn't a very ladylike way to sit back in this time, but Luke was used to her being a bit different, so she knew he wouldn't say anything.

"I came here to be with the only people I'd had in

my life since I was a child. It was always just the three of us. But I don't want to interfere in their new lives. They're starting real families now. I just don't know what I should do. While I'm managing out here all right with everyone else around, the truth is, everything is just so different in this time, I don't know how I would do things on my own. Even washing my clothes is just so difficult from what I'm used to." She laughed softly and shrugged again. "I don't know. It's just hard to know what to do. I guess I'd hoped…"

She stopped talking, not wanting to tell him she'd thought maybe by now she'd have found someone she could build a life with too. Someone to stay here for.

He didn't move, still looking up at the sky as he breathed quietly beside her. "What about Stewart?"

When he finally spoke, his voice startled her. She scrunched her eyes together in confusion and peeked over at him. His face was shaded by his hat, but her heart still lurched at the sight of him. He turned slightly to look at her, and even in the darkness, she could feel his blue eyes piercing into her.

"What about Stewart?" She repeated the question back to him.

"Well, he seems like he'd be someone who could

look after you and give you a good life out here. He's obviously quite taken with you. He seems to be underfoot every time I come around."

She rolled her eyes and looked back out to the darkness. "He might be able to give me a good life, but I'd likely end up punching him in the face long before that could happen. He's nice enough I suppose, and I'm sure will make someone very happy someday. But not me. I don't like people who are arrogant and think they're better than anyone else."

He chuckled low in his throat. "I have to admit, I wouldn't mind seeing him get punched in the face by you. But that's likely not fair because I'm sure he's a decent enough man."

They sat quietly again, and she wondered at how easy it was to just sit like this with someone.

"What about you? What do you plan to do after this trip? You must get tired of doing this, without ever having anywhere to settle."

She held her breath, not liking how much she wanted to hear his reply. Never in her life had she let any man have this much of an influence in her future decisions.

She'd never even kissed Luke, and he'd certainly

never given any impression that there was some-thing between them. So why was she so hopeful that somehow, his answer would affect her own future?

As she let her eyes move over to him, he put his head down and looked at his feet stretched out in front of him. "I've always just made my way, without thinking much about settling. I do what I can to keep myself busy, finding work as I go."

"But you mentioned you were a farmer. Don't you ever miss that?"

"I do. I grew up farming, but then thought I needed to move away to the city to do bigger things." He scoffed and shook his head. "I was young and foolish. Instead of staying and helping my father on the farm, I thought I could show him how much more money there was to be made out in the world." He lifted his eyes back to the sky. "I was starting to realize I'd made a mistake and city life wasn't for me, but then I met Josephine. Blonde hair, delicate as a flower, and she convinced me she loved me, no matter what I did for a living. Until I moved her back out to the farm. She soon realized she'd been wrong about loving me."

"Oh, I'm sure she loved you, Luke. Why else would she have gone with you?"

Her heart ached not only with pain for him, but because it hurt to hear him talking about loving another woman. She sensed, though, that he needed to talk about it, so she let him continue.

"She likely thought she did, for a while. But it wasn't enough. I wasn't enough."

Devyn couldn't imagine the pain he'd felt, and obviously was still working through. Any hope she had that he might be able to move past it all and perhaps have a future with her was gone.

Before she could stop herself, a tear escaped. She hated hearing about his hurt, and she now understood. With a start, she realized she had fallen in love with him, but could never let him know.

He turned his head and their eyes met.

Reaching out, he wiped at her tear, rubbing her skin gently with his calloused thumb. "You've got the most beautiful eyes I've ever seen. What have you done to me, Devyn? Until you came along, I was happy living in my pain."

She gasped with surprise, and he leaned over, pulling her into him as he put his lips on hers. Softly, he moved them over her mouth, still caressing her cheek slowly in circles. His other hand went under her hair, pulling her head closer. She shivered as his fingers moved over the tender skin at the back of her neck, and she found herself grasping at his shirt to hold him tight.

Finally, when she was sure she had forgotten how to breathe, he pulled his head back and looked down into her eyes. He seemed to be searching for something, and she desperately wished she could give it to him.

He sat back and let go of her, looking away as he thrust his fingers into his hair, pushing his hat back from his head. "I'm sorry, Devyn. I shouldn't have done that. I was taking advantage of you, and I apologize."

Her mouth was still hanging open slightly as she tried to get her senses back. She felt so cold now that he'd moved away from her and tugged her shawl closer around her shoulders.

"You don't need to apologize to me, Luke. I'm a big girl. I can make my own decisions about whether I let a man kiss me or not."

He laughed softly, but it sounded sad in the quiet around them. "Yes, I do believe you're capable of making your own decisions. But it just isn't fair to you. I can never give you what you deserve. A home, a family. Someone to love you the way you should be loved."

She could feel anger starting to rise that he

thought he could just make these assumptions on his own. "I'm slowly beginning to see that maybe Stewart isn't the only man out here I'd like to punch in the face." She stood up, ready to get away from him, so she could cry in peace.

But he got up and grabbed her arm, not letting her go. "Devyn, first of all, women don't go around telling men they want to punch them in the face in this time." He tried to pull her closer to him, but she glared at him and held her ground.

"Second, I just can't be with you. And you need to understand that."

She scowled at him angrily. "What did Josephine do to you that made you so against ever finding happiness again? Why do you think you need to be alone forever as punishment? I just don't understand."

His eyes held hers for a second before he closed them. "The last words she ever said to me were that she hoped I never found happiness again. She said I had killed both her and our baby with my selfishness, and that I didn't even deserve a moment of joy again for the rest of my life."

His eyes flickered open, and she could feel the pain in her own heart.

"She knew she was dying, and she told me it was my fault."

In that moment, she knew the pain wrapped around his heart would never let go. He'd decided his dying wife's words were true, and there was nothing she could ever say to make him see otherwise.

Luke made his way around the camp, shaking hands and accepting the words of thanks from the travelers for getting them safely to Oregon City. Some of the families were still grief-stricken over losses they'd had along the way, and he offered his condolences, wishing he could have done more to make sure everyone made it. But everyone who started out in the east knew there would be some casualties, and that was just how things were on the trail.

They'd set up camp last night for the final time in the open meadow along the creek outside the city. Now, everyone would need to decide whether to stay over the winter in tent encampments or hotels, or if they would continue on to their final destinations now to claim the land they'd come out here for.

Today, most would be making their way into the city to stock up and enjoy a taste of civilization again after the months on the trail.

He'd spent the night out here with everyone, making sure everything was finished before heading into town to find a hotel to stay in until he decided where he would be going from here. His eyes kept moving to look toward the wagons where he knew Devyn would be, and he wished he knew what to say when it was time to say goodbye to her. It wasn't going to be easy saying it to any of them, but it was torture knowing how much it would hurt leaving her behind.

After their kiss, he'd found himself thinking so much about Josephine's words again, and the pain he thought he'd managed to bury long ago was now right on the surface. He'd started to believe he could move on and get past the feelings of guilt and responsibility for what happened, but obviously he'd only been fooling himself.

And Devyn deserved much better than he could ever offer her.

"Mr. Bryan, I don't know how I can ever thank you enough for getting us all to Oregon safely. I will always have so many stories to tell little Margaret as she grows about how she came into the world and then her first few weeks of life."

Luke smiled down at the baby Eliza was holding in her arms. Margaret looked up at him with big eyes as though she sensed the importance of her birth and how she'd made it here. "Well, with the start she's had, I'm certain you're going to have your hands full with a strong young lady as she grows up."

Mick laughed and nodded in agreement. "Oh, we're already seeing a stubborn streak in her, so can only imagine what she'll be like as she gets older. But I have a feeling she might end up being just as tough as her namesake, and for that, I will never complain. Knowing she will always be able to take care of herself will ease my worry about her."

Luke's heart lurched slightly at the mention of Devyn, but he had to agree with Mick's assessment of the woman.

"So, have you thought about what you might do for the winter?"

Mick and Eliza shared a smile, before the man answered. "We talked it over, and figure since we've come this far, we may as well get our land settled as soon as possible. I'm going to sign for my parcel today when we go into town, and I'm hoping to find somewhere that won't require too much longer to get to. Then, we'll likely head out first thing tomorrow morning to get started on our new life together. If I can get even a small shelter for us to spend the winter in, then I'll get everything else finished up in the spring."

Eliza laughed and shook her head. "We're both just excited to get settled. I know it would be easier to spend the winter here, but we don't want to wait any longer. As long as we're together, we'll figure things out."

Stewart was standing to the back of the wagon, and he didn't look as excited. "They're being foolish but won't listen to me. So, I'm staying in Oregon City and setting up a practice until my sister comes to her senses and realizes that life just barely surviving isn't what she wants." Thankfully, he must have sensed others didn't really want to listen to what he had to say right now, and he walked away without so much as a thank you to Luke for getting him here.

Eliza took Mick's hand, holding onto Margaret with the other, and smiled warmly up at her husband. "Don't listen to him, Mick. He's the one who has nothing."

"That may be true, but I'm sure getting sick of

hearing it from him. Obviously, he still doesn't believe I can take good care of you, even after all these weeks out here on the trail."

"You're both going to be just fine. I've seen how well you've done, and I have no doubt you'll have a good life out here. There's so much opportunity for anyone willing to put the work in, and I've been around you enough to know you're more than capable." He nodded at Mick, wanting to give the man the reassurance he needed to hear.

"Stewart is just jealous because he hasn't found someone to love him like I have. He thinks life is just about money and possessions, but maybe someday he will find someone to make him realize none of that is important. As long as two people love each other, then nothing else matters. Love will always find a way to provide." Eliza stood up on her toes to place a kiss on Mick's cheek.

Luke wasn't really sure how to offer any more encouragement when his own thoughts had often been no better than Stewart's. He couldn't tell Eliza that sometimes love really wasn't enough. Or that sometimes, just because she thinks everything will be fine now, a day might come when she realizes she was wrong.

He truly hoped in this case it wouldn't happen.

He sensed that Eliza might be a bit stronger than Josephine had been, and she would do whatever she had to do to make things work out.

"I think, in your case, you're absolutely right. You're a lucky man, Mick. You have a good woman who is happy as long as she's with you, and that's more than any money could buy."

As he spoke the words out loud, he started to feel an aching in his chest, as though something was wrong. What had Eliza said about love always finding a way to provide? Maybe it was true, if you were with the right person.

And Devyn wasn't Josephine. She was a strong woman, and he had a feeling nothing would make her give up if it mattered to her.

Had he pushed Devyn away without even giving her a chance, simply because he thought she would be the same as Josephine?

"If you'll excuse me, I need to continue on. But I wish you both well and much happiness. Maybe someday we will cross paths again."

As he hurried over to the wagons where he could see Mary and Minnie sitting, he tried to come up with what he would even say to Devyn. Was he thinking things through enough? Right now, he didn't know what he was going to do. All he knew was that he needed to talk to her, to see if he could figure it out.

When he got up close to them, he could hear Mary crying, while Minnie had her arm around her offering her comfort.

"Is everything all right, ladies?" He crouched down to look at the young girl whose face was blotchy, and her eyes were red from crying.

"No. I love Jasper, and now I'm never going to see him again."

Minnie smiled sadly at him, offering an explanation. "I'm afraid Mary had to say goodbye to her little kitty friend this morning, and she's quite upset."

"Oh no, what happened to Jasper?" He knew Devyn would be devastated at losing the cat.

"Nothing happened to him, really. Just that Devyn took him with her into Oregon City. The men accompanied the women into town, so I offered to stay here with Mary."

So, Devyn must have decided to go straight into the city to stay without even saying goodbye to him.

"Well, I'm sure you can go in and see him again before you all continue traveling to your destination." He knew Hunter and Adam had said they were heading out tomorrow toward Bethany, further south in the Willamette Valley, where they would be settling. But surely her friends would want to stop back in the city to say goodbye to Devyn before they left.

Mary shook her head, tendrils of hair sticking to the wetness of her cheeks. "No, I can't. They said Devyn is leaving today, and where she's going, I won't be able to visit."

A sinking feeling started coiling in his stomach. His eyes lifted to Minnie's, who was nodding sadly. "She's going home, Luke. That's why they all went in with her—to say goodbye. She wanted to see a pioneer town before she goes. But she won't be coming back here."

She was going home. It took him a few seconds to register exactly what that meant.

Where she was going, he couldn't simply ride his horse to find her someday, when he was finally ready.

He had to see her before she left. He had to at least tell her how he felt and see if there was some way she might stay.

Where just a few moments ago, he still wasn't sure what he wanted, he knew now with a certainty that tore at his heart with the knowledge he might be too late.

CHAPTER 18

"Oh, Devyn, I wish you would stay but I'm not going to force you. We both just want you to be happy, and if that means going back home, then we won't stop you." Jenna looped her arm through Devyn's, while Carly did the same on the other side, having to make room for the makeshift cat carrier they'd put together for Jasper to ride in.

Devyn had said her goodbyes to both Hunter and Adam who were picking up some supplies and letting the women have some time together. She hadn't called on Dr. Lachele yet, but she knew when she was ready, all she had to do was say the words and the woman would be here for her.

And, truthfully, she wasn't really sure she was even doing the right thing. While they strolled around the city, with Jasper howling loudly between them, she had to admit she was going to miss the excitement of life out here on the frontier.

She was going back to always being a text or a phone call away at all times of the day or night, social media feeds that never made her feel adequate, and truthfully, just an entire society where she wasn't sure she would even fit in anymore.

Since being back in this time, even though life was much more challenging in many ways, she'd never felt at peace like she did here. Her anxiety was lower, and she loved how everyone just looked out for each other, without question. There wasn't so much focus on what was in it for "me."

But she also knew as a single woman; life was really hard back in these times. She could just go and stay near Jenna and Carly, but she knew deep down, it wasn't fair for them to always need to worry about her too. They would never see it the way she did, but she needed to do what was right.

So, she would go back home and relive the memories of these few weeks, having an experience no one else would ever get.

A sudden crashing sound, followed by loud muttering, came from an alley as they passed, drawing their eyes to the commotion. A woman was tipped over backward on a crate with her feet in the air, a mass of petticoats and fabric covering her head as she fought to stand up.

Carly let go of her arm and raced to the woman, reaching out to take her arm and help her get upright. As the fabric finally dropped down, it revealed a very red in the face Dr. Lachele.

"Oh, for goodness sakes. I tried to pop back here inconspicuously this time and landed right smack in the middle of a bunch of empty crates, in a dusty old back alley, with my feet in the air, and my bloomers showing." She stood up and started vigorously shaking at her skirts. "How in the world does anyone ever get used to wearing all of this fuss?"

All the women laughed, so happy to see the familiar face they'd grown to love. But Devyn also felt a sudden sadness, knowing she was here for her. Obviously, the woman was able to sense when she was needed, so she'd come to get her.

"It's so good to see you, Doctor Lachele. The clothing back here does take some getting used to, and I'm not sure if it's something I'll ever be able to entirely accept. As soon as we get to Bethany, I'm likely going to sit down and make myself some shorts and sundresses to wear around home when no one else will see me." Jenna hugged the woman who'd sent them all here.

Finally, Dr. Lachele locked eyes on Devyn who had stayed back, allowing the other two girls to say hello to her. She would have lots of time hanging out with Dr. Lachele again in book club when she went back.

"So, Devyn, what are we going to do about your situation?"

Of course, she should have known the matchmaker would somehow know exactly what was going on.

"There's really nothing to do, Doctor Lachele. I'm grateful for the chance to have come here, and spend some more time with my friends, but I think it's time for me to go back home."

The woman walked over and brought her eyebrows together. Devyn almost burst out laughing when she saw the purple hair peeking out from beneath the bonnet. While she might think she was being inconspicuous, there's no way Dr. Lachele would ever just "blend in" anywhere.

"Well, Devyn, I'm speaking about the matter with Luke. And I'm sure you already know that."

"I know, but unfortunately things just didn't work out for me with Luke. He's got too much he needs to work through, and I'm never going to try forcing someone to love me. I'm tired of always just hoping for things that aren't meant to be."

"Oh, it's meant to be, Devyn, or I wouldn't have sent you here. Don't you understand how I work?"

"You've done a great job at matching Jenna and Carly, and all of the other people who have left from book club. But surely, even you can admit, not all of them will work out perfectly. I'm okay with it, and not mad or anything. I'm fine with going home and seeing where life takes me."

Dr. Lachele looked at her with her mouth gaping open. "You're *fine* with it? That's what you want for your life? Just *okay and fine*?" She looked back and forth between Jenna and Carly. "And you two were just going to let her go without trying to talk some sense into her?"

"Oh, we tried. But you know how Devyn is once she gets something set in her head." Carly was smirking at her, glad to be on Dr. Lachele's side.

"Well, I don't make mistakes with my matches. There's a reason you're here, and it wasn't just to be with your friends again. Do you not wonder why all your life you were drawn to Luke Bryan? Ever wonder sometimes why the three of you even ended up together in the first place? None of these little things that you likely thought were insignificant were accidents. And you're willing to just throw away all the work of the cosmos…and me…because you want to go back to a life you're *okay* with?"

Devyn stood completely still, letting the woman's words sink in. Is that what she wanted? To settle, for her life?

Jasper howled loudly, letting his displeasure over his current situation be known to everyone around them. Devyn turned to look at Jenna, who put her hands out and took the cat crate from her.

"You've never been one to just settle for anything, Devyn."

"I need to go talk to him one more time. I need to hear it from him that he wants me to leave." She started to turn, noticing the wide grins on all the women's faces.

"What if he says he doesn't want you to leave?"

Luke's voice reached her ears before she noticed him standing in front of her, and she almost ran straight into his chest. The sun behind him was making it hard to see his face, so she brought her hand up to shield her eyes, wanting to see his eyes as he spoke.

"We're going to take a little walk and leave you two alone. I'll still be here, Devyn, if you have need of me. But be sure you're making the right decision." Dr. Lachele looped arms with her friends and led them away. "Now, you two ladies can show me around this frontier town. Maybe we can see some good-looking cowboys."

Devyn watched them go, suddenly feeling unsure. What was she supposed to tell him? Should she just blurt out that she loved him and wanted to stay here with him, but she wasn't going to beg for his love in return?

He reached out and took her hand, turning her back around and leading her into the alley, away from the bustle on the sidewalks around them.

When they stopped, he faced her, taking her other hand in his. She held her breath, having so much she wanted to say but afraid to say even a word.

"Devyn, when I heard you were leaving for good, and going back where you came from, I have no words to describe the pain I felt. I can't go through that again. When I lost Josephine and my baby, I wanted to die with them. I didn't believe I ever deserved to live a happy life after that. And I've carried her words with me every day since, determined to punish myself for something beyond my control."

He swallowed, his blue eyes never wavering from her face. She was having trouble concentrating as his thumbs moved in slow circles on her own.

"I don't have a lot to offer you if you stay, but I'd sure like it if you would consider it. I will do my best to give you a good life, even if it might not be easy. And I know I don't deserve—"

She shook her head, cutting him off. "Luke, I love you."

His mouth was still open slightly, but a smile started to spread across his face. "I love you too, Devyn. And I can't believe how lucky I am to hear you say those words to me. I was worried I was going to be too late. But can I ask you to stay if I can't give you everything you could ever dream of? I have some money put away. We could start a little farm—"

She held his hands firmly and smiled up at him, hoping he could see all the love in her eyes as she cut him off once more. "If you love me, I already have everything I could ever dream of."

And with those words, he brought his lips down on hers, his arms going around her back and pulling her in close, giving her no doubt, he never planned on letting her go.

Loud clapping and cheering sounded behind

them, and Luke lifted his head with a groan. He let her turn around, keeping an arm around her shoulders as they faced their audience.

Dr. Lachele came over and curtsied clumsily with her overflowing skirts, grinning at them both. "As I've said many, *many* times—Doctor Lachele never makes a mistake when it comes to love."

"I think Jasper is taking his new role as protector of this new little friend very seriously." Devyn laughed as the tomcat gently placed his paw on the baby who Jenna was reaching down to take from her arms. Jasper hadn't left the baby's side since she was born yesterday.

Devyn had given birth to a little girl with the help of her friends and, of course, her husband. Luke had been a wreck, though, and hadn't really been much help, but she'd insisted he stay right by her, so he knew everything was going okay.

But when Nora Lachele Bryan had arrived safely, and loudly into the world, he hadn't stopped grinning since.

She still couldn't believe it had been a whole year

since they'd arrived in Oregon. She and Luke had married in Oregon City the same day they'd declared their love for each other and had followed the others to the small town of Bethany. Of course, it really wasn't considered small anymore, not with the amount of people who had been settling there over the past few years. And Devyn knew in her heart she would never find another place as welcoming, which accepted them all into the community so easily.

They'd made many friends since arriving, and Devyn had no doubt she was going to be very happy here for the rest of her life. Luke had signed for a parcel of land right next to Hunter's, and while the homes they'd built weren't grand by modern standards, Devyn had never lived anywhere that felt more like a home.

Eliza and Mick had ended up coming with them, and they were already expecting another baby in the next few months.

Adam and Jenna built a home right in town, and Adam was back at work as a blacksmith with his cousin, Connor. Everyone had found their happiness at the end of the trail.

Both Carly and Jenna had given birth to daughters in the past few months, so the three friends were ecstatic knowing their girls would all grow up with a strong friendship like their mothers had. It was like it was meant to be, and Devyn thought back to what Dr. Lachele had said about nothing being an accident.

Through her entire life, all she'd ever wanted was a family, and now she knew without a doubt in her mind, this was the family she'd always been destined for. The friends she'd had back home, and now the extended group of friends she'd made on the trail, and right here in Bethany.

There might not be any DNA shared between them, but they were her heart family, and she knew that was even stronger than blood.

Luke came over and pulled a chair up next to her, putting his arm around her shoulders as she leaned her head into his shoulder.

"You really should be having a rest while you have all these people here to help look after Nora. You don't want to end up sick."

She smiled, relaxing into his embrace as she looked around at the people filling their small home.

Mary had moved over beside her on the settee now and was trying to comfort Jasper who was not happy with his new baby being taken away. Jenna and Carly were arguing over who they thought Nora looked the most like out of them both. It seemed they'd forgotten they weren't actually related, so should have claim to some of the features on the baby's face.

Minnie had come too and was standing at Devyn's small cupboard making a feast for everyone to enjoy. At the moment, she was scolding Gordon who was sitting right next to her, waiting for any scrap to fall to the floor. Beside her, Eliza helped to roll out some dough, her protruding belly making it difficult to get close enough to the counter. Mick came over, placing his hand on her back and leaned down to rub it gently, helping to get out any knots from the extra weight she was carrying.

The men sat talking as they held their own daughters, seeming to be unaware of the chaos of everyone around them. It had become a normal occurrence, with so many of them getting together all the time, no one really noticed the noise anymore.

For three girls who grew up without homes, or families, they'd settled into this life joyfully, knowing it was where they were meant to be.

"I don't need any rest, Luke. I'm just so full of happiness right now, here like this, I don't want it to ever end."

Luke laughed as he listened to her friends now

arguing over whose turn it was to hold the baby. "Oh, I have a feeling these moments aren't going to be ending any time soon. This little makeshift family we've gathered around us don't seem to have any plans of going anywhere."

She lifted her eyes to his and smiled up at him, hoping he could see the love she was feeling.

"Thank you."

He stared down at her, a confused expression on his face. "You're thanking me? After you just gave me the most beautiful little daughter I could have ever hoped for? And you showed me how to forgive myself and finally settle down, letting go of the guilt that had driven me for so many years." He leaned down and placed a kiss on her lips. "No, I'm the one who should be thanking you."

She laughed softly and held onto his shirt so he couldn't pull back.

"Maybe, but you've given me all of that and more. You've given me everything I'd ever dreamed of having. I hope you know just how much I love you."

"As much as the real Luke Bryan?" His blue eyes sparkled as he grinned down at her.

She tipped her head back and laughed. She'd shared her secret love about the other man with him, and they'd often listened to his music saved on her phone.

"I think I love you even more."

They shared another kiss, the sounds of their newfound family talking and laughing around them in the background, filling both of their hearts with joy.

I hope you enjoyed reading, Devyn's Dream. If you could take a couple minutes and head back to the retailer you purchased from to leave a review, it would be greatly appreciated :)

USA Today Bestselling Author, Kay P. Dawson writes sweet western romance - the kind that leaves out all of the juicy details and immerses you in a true, heartfelt love story. Growing up pretending she was Laura Ingalls, she's always had a love for the old west and pioneer times. She believes in true love, and finding your happy ever after.

Happily married mom of two girls, Kay has always taught her children to follow their dreams. And, after a breast cancer diagnosis at the age of 39, she realized it was time to take her own advice. She had always wanted to write a book, and she decided that the someday she was waiting for was now.

She writes western historical, contemporary and time travel romance that all transport the reader to a time or place where true love always finds a way.

You can connect with Kay through her website at **KayPDawson.com**

**She also has an active fan group where she

hangs out with her readers…**https://www.facebook.com/groups/kaypdawsonfans/**

****Newsletter SignUp:**

https://www.kaypdawson.com/newsletter

****Bookbub Follow:**

https://www.bookbub.com/authors/kay-p-dawson

kaypdawsonwrites@gmail.com